UNDER THE MISTLETOE

By the time Chastity was standing under the mistletoe, her half boots were caked with mud. She tried to stand on tiptoe, straining to reach the elusive greenery, but her feet bogged deeper and deeper into the muck. Her feet were stuck fast to the ground. She bent down and began to unlace her half boots.

With one foot free, she stood like a flamingo for a moment, unwilling to put her stockinged foot down in the mud.

"May I be of assistance, Madam?"

Chastity whirled around, almost losing her precarious balance.

The voice belonged to a tall, ruggedly handsome man, and she blushed and silently wished him at the devil. Then she frowned. There was something familiar about his roguish face, his intense hazel eyes. She noted his elegant dress, a riding ensemble of the first stare.

There was no horse in sight, a query she immediately put to the stranger.

"I don't ride—not anymore," he replied with a smile, tapping a cane against his leg. "But I like to think I can still be of assistance to a damsel in distress, especially one as beautiful as you."

Chastity pursed her lips and rolled her eyes.

Alex looked at the tree and asked, "The mistletoe, was it?"

She nodded, and he pulled down the mistletoe. But before Chastity could take it, Alex stretched out one long, strong arm, holding the greenery above their heads. "A forfeit first, I think," he murmured, and bent his head to hers . . .

An Improper Pursuit
Donna Bell

ZEBRA BOOKS
KENSINGTON PUBLISHING CORP.

ZEBRA BOOKS are published by

Kensington Publishing Corp.
475 Park Avenue South
New York, NY 10016

First Printing: June, 1994

Printed in the United States of America

*For my daughters Jamie and Tiffany
and my son Stuart*

Chapter One

"Chastity! Where do you think you're going? And dressed like that, too!"

Chastity grimaced before turning around to face her mother. She pasted a smile on her features as she responded mildly, "I am dressed this way to fetch the mistletoe, Mother."

"Surely a groom or footman . . ."

"Certainly, but I will still have to go, to make certain they choose the prettiest."

Lady Hartford paused, cocking her head to one side, causing her still-golden curls to bob entrancingly, a habit she had cultivated in her first Season.

"Very well," she began, and her daughter breathed a silent sigh of relief. But it was premature. "First, however, a word with you in private."

Her mother looked about the spacious kitchen and pointed to the larder. Chastity followed her inside and closed the door. Her mother stretched out a plump hand and smoothed a stray brown curl away from her daughter's brow.

"If you will persist in going out without a hat, your skin will soon be as brown as your hair."

At Chastity's raised brow, (how many times had they had this same conversation?), her mother said hastily,

"But that is not what I wished to speak to you about. Our guests will begin arriving soon. There will be several eligible bachelors among them. While I know you have no interest in such matters, I hope you will be careful in your behavior—for your sisters' sakes. This will be their first entree into polite society. With their beauty and grace, they might both be betrothed before their first Season!"

Chastity's face remained a mask of courteous attention as her mother's enthusiasm bubbled forth. How well Chastity remembered her own Season in London, the sighs of disappointment, the clucks of disapproval each time she modeled a new gown for her mother. She took a deep breath and put the memories away. At four and twenty, the pain and anger had dissipated. She wouldn't allow herself to dwell on it.

"So Chastity," concluded her mother, "you won't do anything to give our guests a . . . a disgust of the family?"

Chastity opened her green eyes to their widest, most innocent gaze—a habit her mother deplored, considering it too forward—and smiled sweetly. "I wouldn't dream of it!" She turned and, with hand on the latch, asked, "Was there anything else, Mother?"

"No, no," said Lady Hartford, wringing her handkerchief nervously. "Just do hurry back so you can change."

"Of course, Mother."

Then Chastity escaped out the kitchen door, striding purposefully along the path through the kitchen garden, knowing her mother would be watching, disgruntled. A small foxhound fell into step behind her. When she was out of sight of the house, Chastity slowed her pace.

The sun was shining for the first time in two weeks. The ground was saturated from the heavy rains; the dampness wet the hem of her gown as she crossed the green meadow. When she entered the thick woods, she had to choose her way carefully, hopping daintily from one tuft of grass to the next.

"We shall both be in the doghouse, Buster, if we get muddy," she said, looking down at the hound beside her. He cocked his head to one side, and she shook a finger at him. "None of that, my lad. You remind me of you-know-who." He answered with a quick yip and a wag of the tail.

She looked ahead at the spreading oak tree, its branches dipping close to the ground. The shade had robbed the ground underneath of all vegetation, leaving only a few old leaves and a mass of mud.

"Stay, Buster." The dog settled down on its haunches while Chastity set out across the mud. On a recent amble she had seen a large clump of mistletoe on one of the lower branches. She was sure she could reach it. By the time she was standing under the mistletoe, her half boots were caked with mud, raising her five-foot-eight-inch frame even higher. She tried to stand on tiptoe, straining to reach the elusive greenery, but her feet bogged deeper and deeper into the muck.

I didn't realize it was so high, she thought crossly as she pulled away a few sprigs before losing her balance and swaying dangerously. She would either have to climb the tree—something she would have loved to do in her tomboy days—or jump. Chastity considered each choice doubtfully. She gathered herself to spring up and grab the mistletoe.

"Ohhh!" she yelled as she sprang up only to lose her balance and fall, catching herself with one hand on the muddy ground. She managed to straighten, grumbling softly as she realized her feet were stuck fast to the ground. She bent down and began to unlace her half boots.

With one foot free, she stood like a flamingo for a

moment, unwilling to put her stockinged foot down in the mud.

"May I be of assistance, Madam?"

Chastity whirled around, almost losing her precarious balance.

The voice belonged to a tall, ruggedly handsome man, and she blushed and silently wished him at the devil. Then she frowned. There was something familiar about his roguish face, his intense hazel eyes. His hair was a dark brown, almost black, and it was carelessly combed. She noted his elegant dress, a riding ensemble of the first stare.

There was no horse in sight, a query she immediately put to the stranger who was attempting to brush muddy paw prints from his shiny hessians.

"You are most observant. Down, animal."

"His name is Buster."

"Then down, Buster. And no, I don't ride—not anymore," he replied with a smile, tapping a cane against his leg. "But I like to think I can still be of assistance to a damsel in distress, especially one as beautiful as you."

Chastity pursed her lips and rolled her eyes.

He noted her displeasure and said quite sensibly, "Alexander Fitzsimmons, at your service."

"Alex Fitzsimmons!" she squeaked. "What are you doing here?"

At this, a wide grin of recognition spread across the gentleman's face, and he said amiably, "Chastity Hartford? How good to see you again."

Chastity's complexion turned a ruddy color as she realized who her would-be rescuer was. It had been ten years since she had seen him; still, the embarrassing remembrance of her girlhood infatuation washed over her like it was yesterday.

Alex Fitzsimmons ignored her embarrassment and

strode across the mud, putting his hands on her waist, trying to pick her up.

Chastity shook her head, pushing away from him, and he had to grasp her hands to steady her.

"I'm stuck," she explained grudgingly.

Alex bent down and lifted her skirts ever so slightly. "Well and truly," he acknowledged as he began to unlace her other boot.

Chastity stared ahead, one hand resting lightly on his muscular shoulder to retain her balance while she tried to ignore the rush of sensations his touch sent dancing through her. She had heard people say they were mortified—now she understood the feeling perfectly.

Suddenly he stood up, practically threw her over his shoulder, and carried her to a small patch of sunshine beyond the oak tree. Buster assured himself of his mistress's good health by barking and jumping up onto her skirt.

"Down," said Alex sternly, and the hound subsided, his tail wagging furiously.

"I am so sorry to have caused you to muddy your boots," said Chastity.

"Think nothing of it. I will change as soon as I arrive."

"Arrive? But your godparents no longer live in this neighborhood."

"No, but I've been invited to your house party." With a sly wink, he added, "I was sure you had a hand in that."

"Certainly not!" she snapped. "My mother didn't tell me who was invited. And I certainly never dreamed you would be included!"

"I am devastated," he said weakly.

Chastity expelled an unladylike snort.

Alex looked back at the tree and asked, "The mistletoe, was it?"

She nodded, and he retraced his steps, pulled down the mistletoe, and returned quickly to her side, presenting it with a bow.

Before Chastity could take it, Alex stretched out one long, strong arm, holding the greenery above their heads. Then he paused, his hazel eyes resting on Chastity's lips. Her eyes grew wide.

"A forfeit first, I think," he murmured, and bent his head to hers. Taking her face in one hand, he let his lips touch hers.

Chastity's eyes drooped closed; shocked at first, she swayed against him, weak-kneed. Alex dropped the mistletoe, and his arm encircled her waist. His touch made Chastity snap back to reality, and she pushed away roughly.

Alex watched her in silence as she scrubbed her lips with the back of her hand, swooped down to gather up the forgotten mistletoe, and sprinted barefoot through the woods, her dog at her heels.

Alex's pent-up breath made a whooshing sound, and he shook himself mentally. This was not what had brought him to Folkestone. He would have to be on guard against such foolishness. He grinned—his own foolishness.

Picking up Chastity's mud-caked half boots and retrieving his cane, he headed toward the house, whistling carelessly.

"Argh!" screamed Lady Hartford as she rounded the corner and glimpsed her eldest daughter's disarray. Then the petite matron, after a lightning glance behind her for her maid, gracefully swooned. Her maid laid her gently on the floor and quickly produced smelling salts to revive her stricken mistress.

Chastity observed all of this dispassionately. Her mother revived and moaned weakly, "Why, why?"

"Heavens, Mother. It's not the end of the world; I will change."

"But the guests are arriving. What if someone were to see you? Why, Fitzsimmons's curricle just arrived. And where are your shoes?"

Chastity bit back a scathing comment and said, "If you'll excuse me, Mother, I'll make myself presentable." She bobbed a quick curtsey and hurried to her room.

Once behind the safety of her closed door, Chastity rang for hot water and began stripping off her wet stockings, her muddy gown following instantly. She looked up, catching sight of her reflection in the long cheval glass, noted for the first time the smudge of mud on her cheek, and tossed her head defiantly before putting on her wrapper.

After bathing, and washing her unfashionably long hair, she sat in front of the fire and brushed the shining tresses until they were dry. The dressing bell sounded, and Chastity stood up automatically and went through the dressing room door.

This room was situated between Chastity's bedroom and the one her twin sisters shared. It was a narrow room, lined with hooks holding dozens of gowns, mostly in soft pastels, making it look like a rainbow.

Her twin sisters were there already, chattering about the guests and their prospects as they selected their gowns for dinner. Their maid Rosey gathered petticoats and stockings.

"What did you think of Sir Charles? Wasn't he droll?" said Tranquility. "Mama says his pockets are to let. Lady Ravenwood told her so; she was furious."

"True, but I think Lord Ravenwood is the best catch," said Sincerity knowingly.

"I saw Fitzsimmons arrive. His prospects are not bad, and he is so-o-o handsome," enthused Tranquility.

"I do not think him so very handsome," interjected Chastity as she pulled out a modest lavender gown.

The younger girls exchanged winks and gathered around her.

"How do you know, Chastity?"

"Were you spying on him in the salon? I didn't think you'd be so brazen," said Sincerity.

"You can't possibly be acquainted with him, since Mama says he is only just home from the Peninsula."

Chastity turned a dull red, just as her sisters knew she would. Her voice squeaked as she tried for a haughty tone, saying, "I happened to look out of the window as he arrived, that is all. But you are welcome to your own opinion and to him, for that matter." She fled to her room, but the younger girls pursued her, protesting vehemently.

"We're sorry, Chastity; we were only teasing," said Tranquility, who always spoke first.

"Yes, Chastity, please don't be upset. We didn't mean to hurt your feelings!" said Sincerity.

Chastity smiled at them. They really were sweet girls though their names were sadly inappropriate. Sincerity enjoyed nothing better than embroidering a story until it bore little resemblance to the truth. And Tranquility's presence often signaled an end to peace and quiet.

"Never mind. I know you meant no harm, but we had best hurry if we are to be downstairs on time."

With this, the twins scurried back to their own room, their laughter and chatter floating through the open doors. Chastity crossed the room and shut her door softly.

Sometimes, she felt as if she had been placed in the wrong setting, with the wrong family. Her father, of course, was the exception. He was a sensible man, not given to frivolity, and he was kind. His dry wit matched Chastity's, but their repartee only bored her mother and sisters. The problem was that he left all decisions regarding his three daughters to his wife. It was not an uncommon arrangement, but it distressed Chastity who was as unlike her mother as fire was to snow.

Her mother and sisters were petite, rounded, and soft, with golden curls. Chastity's hair was brown, and she was tall and slender, though her mother described her as ungainly. The twins and her mother were silly and frivolous, interested only in fashion and society. Chastity was serious, witty, almost—her mother often warned—a bluestocking. But most of all, Tranquility and Sincerity were marriageable, and she was not.

Chastity sat down abruptly at the dressing table and dragged a comb through her long curls. It brought tears to her eyes, and she dashed them away angrily.

She looked at her image and said, "And what do you do but throw yourself at the first man you see! Won't they enjoy that scandal! They'll say, 'Chastity—what an inappropriate name for that girl!' "

With a resolute jutting of her jaw, she finished her toilette and went down the stairs, more determined than ever to melt into the wallpaper.

The salon was still empty when she entered, and Chastity chose the grouping of chairs at the far end of the room, considering this area to be well away from any attractions. She had no idea who their guests were, except the few gentlemen whom her sisters had mentioned. Her mother hadn't considered it to be of importance to consult her eldest daughter on the guest list, and she hadn't asked. She had been told only that Lord and Lady Costain were coming, bringing along Lady Costain's spinster sister, Miss Emma Bishop, an old school friend of Chastity's.

Her mother and father entered the salon and advanced toward her.

"Good evening, my dear. You look charming," said her father gallantly.

Chastity brightened. Her father was a tall man of some fifty years, his figure still trim and his hair thinning gracefully. Chastity had always considered her father as the ideal of manhood and wondered how her mother could seem so indifferent to him. Other ladies recognized his charm, but her mother preferred to order him around, dismissing his remarks as nonsense.

"Thank you, Papa," she responded. "You and Mother are looking very elegant."

"You like my new coat? Picked it up in London only last week. Weston, of course," he added with a wink.

"It's very nice."

"Never mind your silliness, Herbert. Chastity, I'm afraid I have bad news," said Lady Hartford dramatically. "Our numbers are uneven. If only I had been warned, I wouldn't have invited the Rector to join us! It's all Lady Costain's doing; she knew how it would be!"

"I'm sure you can manage one extra guest, dear," said Lord Hartford calmly.

"But it was so inconsiderate! Imagine! Emma Bishop betrothed at her age! And the man! Why, I would never include such a dull, common . . ."

"Watch yourself, Divinity," warned her husband.

"What's this? Emma is to be married? How wonderful!" said Chastity, genuinely pleased for her friend.

Her mother dropped her voice and said confidentially, "Rather sudden, as I understand it from her brother-in-law. It makes one wonder . . ."

"Nonsense, Divinity! And shame on Costain for spreading rumors! I suspect he's only sorry to lose his free housekeeper."

"Herbert, Lord Costain is a very distinguished gentleman. And he is our guest." With this, Lady Hartford hurried to welcome Lady Ravenwood.

She missed her husband's ironic comment, "So is Miss Bishop." Then he seated himself beside Chastity to watch the unfolding tableau, saying, "This should prove to be a most entertaining house party. A little taste of the London Season next spring."

"What do you mean, Papa?"

"Well, the whole purpose of this gathering is to give the twins a preview of London mores and behaviors. Just look at the guest list."

"I don't even know who's here," said Chastity.

"Then let me fill you in. We have Lord and Lady Costain. He is, as you know, a friend of mine from the House of Lords; his wife is, ah, not a friend. She and your mother should be interesting to watch. Your friend Emma and her new fiancé are unexceptional. Then there is Ruben; I insisted he be invited. No sense him spending Christmas alone up in Leicestershire. Next, we have Cousin Virgil; least said, best," he added, exchanging a grin with his favorite daughter. "Then there is your Aunt Lavinia, here to give your mother moral support, I suppose, but a more useless female I have yet to encounter. I doubt we will even know she's about. After that there is Lady Ravenwood; a regular tartar, but a leader of the *Ton*. Your mother had to include her in order to get the grandson, a silly twit if I ever saw one. But he's as rich as Golden Ball, and that makes him acceptable to your mother. Sir Charles is a puzzle; I can only guess that your mother thinks his old aunt is going to die soon—though I think she is too mean for that— and that he will be towed out of River Tick where he constantly finds himself."

"The twins were saying Lady Ravenwood told mother that Sir Charles was all to pieces," said Chastity.

"I tried to tell her, too, but you know how that is. Finally we get to Alex; you should remember him. I came across him in London and invited him. Your mother took some persuading, but when I told her of his two estates and the townhouse in London, she came about."

"Is he so wealthy?"

"Wealthy enough. I think she has him in mind for Tranquility. We'll see. The man's seen a bit of the world; I doubt a chit of seventeen will hold much attraction for him. Speak of the devil."

"Mr. Fitzsimmons, we are so delighted you could join us," gushed Lady Hartford. "Have you met my daughters? Ah, here they are now."

Alex turned and watched as Tranquility and Sincerity floated into the room. They were beautiful girls. They wore identical sprig muslin gowns. Tranquility's was trimmed with knots of blue ribbons; Sincerity's, with pink.

"No, my lady, I haven't had that pleasure. Though I should know them anywhere; they are so like you. And it is easy to see where they come by their loveliness." He delivered these compliments with an elegant bow which sent the twins into paroxysms of giggles—not of the irritating ilk, but a soft, trilling melody perfected by hours of practice.

"This is Tranquility, and this is Sincerity," said her ladyship proudly.

"And your other daughter?" asked Alex.

"Chastity? She's here somewhere. Oh, Lord and Lady Costain, come in, come in. Let me introduce you to Mr. Fitzsimmons."

And with this, Chastity was forgotten, her father called to heel by her mother, and the tedious evening begun.

Chastity welcomed Emma Bishop's entrance, but it was soon evident that her old friend was wrapped up with her betrothed, a quiet, hawk-faced man who looked sadly out of place. Though Miss Bishop took the empty space beside Chastity on the sofa, she spoke only to her Mr. Peaches, who had taken a straight-backed chair and placed it next to her, his bony knees almost touching hers.

It was with relief that Chastity greeted Petrie's dinner announcement. It was with dismay that she found herself seated between the local rector and one of their least interesting guests, her mother's Cousin Virgil, a complete fop who dyed the palms of his hands pink with cochineal and wore the most appalling waistcoats. He was at least forty years old, lived in London, and boasted of having not two thoughts to rub together. It was not an idle boast, thought Chastity.

After a brief, civil greeting, Virgil turned his back on her and concentrated on Lady Costain on his left. Chastity stared at the soup in the shallow china bowl before her and grimaced.

She looked down the long table to see her sisters twittering—in a charming manner—first with one dinner partner, then the other. On Sincerity's right was Lord Ravenwood, a silly, but handsome young man. Between the girls was a man Chastity had met briefly named Sir Charles Davenport. He was a handsome, devil-may-care Corinthian who was charming both her sisters with his wit. On Tranquility's other side sat Alex Fitzsimmons. Though he didn't ignore Lady Ravenwood to his left, he was much more attentive to Tranquility. And who could blame him, thought Chastity, watching her sisters. Both girls were pretty and lively—perfect products of a perfect upbringing, suited for enchanting and ensnaring the gentlemen. With an audible sniff, Chastity let her eyes roam to the far end of the table where she discovered her mother fixing her with a baleful stare.

Chastity turned immediately, smiled at the aged rector on her right and said, "How are the plans for the Christmas pageant going, Mr. Wright?"

Reluctantly, the old man turned away from his plate and said forcefully, "What?"

The footmen began to remove the soup bowls; more footmen came in to serve up the next course of Poulet Provençal, stewed tomatoes and sautéed mushrooms. Although the servants proceeded in near silence, the confusion made conversation more challenging.

When Chastity repeated her query, the rector said even more loudly, "What? You must learn to speak up, Miss Chastity."

"I . . . said . . . how . . . are . . . the . . . preparations . . . for . . . the . . . Christmas . . . pageant . . . going?" At his pronounced frown, Chastity took a deep breath and repeated loudly and precisely, "CHRISTMAS PAG-EANT!"

With dawning horror, Chastity glanced beyond the rector's face, down the row of silent, staring diners, to her mother, who looked apoplectic, and then across the wide table where the other guests were tittering, covering their mouths and winking at one another as they stared at her.

Her first instinct was to flee—a social solecism. Then she realized her dinner companion had launched into a loud, elaborate dissertation on the pageant. Escape was impossible; she couldn't leave him open to more ridicule. She wished she could fade into the woodwork; to be the center of attention, the butt of the joke, was her worst nightmare.

"Indeed, Miss Tranquility, it is a wonderful sight. You must allow me the privilege of escorting you to the opera next spring." Everyone's eyes turned to the speaker with the resonant tones.

Tranquility smiled brightly, took her cue, and said distinctly, "I look forward to it, Mr. Fitzsimmons."

And suddenly, everyone at the table was speaking out, forgetting their usual hushed dinner table tones. In the general hubbub, Chastity looked across the table, her eyes shining with gratitude, and raised her glass to her savior. With a charming smile, Alex returned the gesture before turning to speak to Tranquility again.

The volume of general conversation made speaking to the rector impossible, so Chastity concentrated on her meal, counting the minutes until she could escape to the solitude of her room.

First, her mother would rise and signal the ladies it was time to leave the gentlemen to their port. Next, Chastity would be required to play the pianoforte—softly, so as not to disturb conversation. Then the gentlemen would rejoin the ladies, and she could find a quiet corner while Sincerity and Tranquility impressed the male guests with their musical talents. Finally, the tea tray would arrive. Afterwards, she could escape.

With the evening "agenda" foremost in her mind, Chastity calmed down, patience being one of her virtues.

Over the trifle, she raised her deep, green eyes, certain someone was staring at her, and encountered Alex Fitzsimmons' hazel ones. She noted one brow slightly arched, one corner of his sensuous mouth curving upward, ever-so-slightly. Her stomach fluttered, and her fork clattered against the plate, earning another reproving glance from her mother. Chastity lowered her eyes to her plate.

She was grateful to him, of course, for saving her from that embarrassing incident with the rector. But did he have to stare at her so? He was probably remembering that unpardonable kiss in the woods—something a true gentleman would never do. He had taken advantage of their situation; surely he couldn't blame her for it.

Chastity swallowed the bite of trifle she had taken. She could feel the blood creeping up her chest, flushing her skin with a ruddy tint. She thanked heaven she preferred high necklines, and then began to think of other things to stem the rising blush. But it was impossible, knowing he was watching her, invading her thoughts. A bright red staining her cheeks as she recalled her response to his kiss, she chanced a quick glimpse.

Anger replaced embarrassment as she realized Fitzsimmons was once again deep in conversation with her sister. His glance in her direction had been only that—a fleeting look—nothing more. Her foolishness, her romanticism, had been allowed to rule her thoughts once again, and her anger turned inward.

Chastity returned to her trifle and wondered how her mother could serve a dish that had absolutely no taste.

Dinner ended and the ladies retired. Alex watched his dinner partner smile coyly at him, and he tried to restrain his impatience.

This was not going to work! How could he possibly investigate anything with twin clinging vines attached to him at every waking moment? He would have to withdraw and inform the Home Office . . .

"Alex? Which will it be?"

Alex looked up at his old friend Sir Charles and indicated the Madeira.

"How was your trip down, Fitzsimmons?" asked Lord Hartford.

"Uneventful, which is the best one can hope for, I suppose," he replied with a languid wave of his hand as though taking a poll amongst his fellow travelers, who murmured their general agreement.

"Changed much?" came the next query.

Alex took a sip and looked up at the older man. What did he mean by that? Was there some hidden meaning? Had he heard about Alex's jaunt through the woods?

Did Hartford feel threatened by it? Alex decided to take it at face value and answered, "Not your place, my lord. Now my godparents' old estate appears to be going to wrack and ruin."

Lord Hartford nodded. "It stood empty too long while their heirs bickered over what to do with it. I was glad to see it occupied again, even by a Frenchie."

Alex feigned surprise and said, "A Frenchman? I had no idea. Of course, I didn't go up to the door."

"An émigrée," said Lord Hartford with a wink at everyone. "And a lovely one, at that."

"What is her name?" said Sir Charles with growing interest.

"La Comtesse de St. Pierre."

"A countess, eh? Probably poor as a church mouse like most of the Frenchies that fled France in the past decade," said Sir Charles whose interest was purely mercenary; everyone knew he had to find an heiress to restore his fortunes.

"Not if appearances are any indication. She has a staff of servants and she is putting the place in order—slowly, to be sure, but she's already made a number of improvements, I'm told."

"I spoke to the gatekeeper. He's French, too," said Alex, hoping to keep the subject going. The information the Home Office had supplied him with was scanty. Perhaps this French countess's presence in the neighborhood was only a coincidence, perhaps not. But it was enough to make him suspicious of her. And if she was involved, she might have accomplices in the area. Alex looked up at Lord Hartford with narrowed eyes.

"Too many of 'em there, if you ask me," his host was saying. "I can't like it, of course, but there's nothing I can do."

"Will we get to meet the countess?" asked Sir Charles.

"Lady Hartford will no doubt include her in some of the festivities," said his lordship. "Virgil, have another glass of this port. Tell me what you think of it."

Thus addressed, the effeminate Virgil puffed out his chest, filled his cheeks with the potent liquid, and pursed his lips. After swallowing, he pronounced grandly, "Quite nice, Hartford, quite. Not as good as what I've had from old Ponsonby's cellars, but very creditable."

Lord Hartford thanked his pompous guest and said, "Time to rejoin the ladies, eh?"

Amid the general movement toward the door, Lord Hartford put his hand on Alex's shoulder and said quietly, "A word with you, my boy."

Alex waited expectantly. Had he given something away? Did Hartford have knowledge of his mission? But Hartford's next words put to rest this suspicion instantly.

"About Chastity. I want to thank you for helping her out of that sticky situation."

"Think nothing of it, my lord. I would have done the same for anyone," he said, reflecting that it was the second "sticky situation" he had saved Chastity from that day.

Alex reached for the door, but a hand on his sleeve restrained him. "Yes, my lord?"

"Fitzsimmons, I hesitate to bring you into this. To ask you . . ."

Alex's muscles tensed. So there was some connection between Hartford and his mission. But which side was Hartford on? The Home Office had warned him to trust no one.

"It's about my daughter."

Alex frowned. Where was the man going with this strange conversation?

"Chastity?" he prompted.

"My wife has planned a scavenger hunt to entertain

our guests. You young men will be paired off with the young ladies."

"It sounds amusing," said Alex doubtfully. Also time consuming, he groaned inwardly. That was all he needed, a female attached to his side every time he left his room.

"Amusing for some," said the older man with a grimace. "The thing is, I know my wife. She'll pair Chastity with Virgil or Ruben—who's old enough to be her father. Even young Ravenwood would be a disaster. He's so silly; Chastity would have no patience with him. And he'd probably sulk because he would want one of the other girls. They're just as silly as he is."

"That's interesting, my lord, but why tell me?" said Alex, barely restraining his impatience.

Lord Hartford produced a small piece of paper from his pocket and handed it to Alex.

He unfolded it and read, "Chastity." He frowned, his eyes asking a question.

"I took it out of the ginger jar my wife fixed for the drawing. When it's your turn to draw, you can produce Chastity's name."

Another kind of suspicion, perhaps foreboding, descended on Alex.

It must have shown in his eyes, for Lord Hartford added bluntly, "No, I'm not matchmaking. I just want Chastity to have a pleasant holiday. If her friend weren't so wrapped up with that new fiancé, I wouldn't interfere. You showed her that one kindness; I thought perhaps you wouldn't mind, that's all."

Alex hesitated, then a wicked grin lit his face. By going along with Hartford, he could frustrate the domineering Lady Hartford, thwart the clinging twins, and, recalling Chastity's aversion to his kiss, irritate his scavenger hunt partner sufficiently that she would avoid his company entirely.

"You needn't answer me now," said Lord Hartford. "Just think on it. We'd better rejoin the others or my wife will be suspecting collusion."

Alex slipped the paper into his pocket and followed his host down the corridor. The long salon was filled with music. Sincerity sat at the pianoforte while Sir Charles stood beside her turning the pages of the music. Tranquility smiled brightly at Alex and patted the empty seat beside her on the sofa. Alex smiled and joined her.

Tranquility used her fan to advantage, tapping Alex's arm playfully, then unfurling it and peeping over the top in a charming manner.

Alex was unmoved. He couldn't say why. After spending four years in the Peninsula, he should feel something. He had dreamed of being civilized again, surrounded by the incredibly civilizing influence of English ladies in their delicate dresses. The reality, however, struck him as tedious. A wave of impatience washed over him. He had been given an assignment; he had little interest in the vagaries of polite society. Four years of fighting, following orders, and doing his duty had changed him. He merely wanted to get on with the work at hand.

His eyes traveled to the far end of the room where Chastity sat alone. Not alone, precisely. The rector sat beside her, his gentle snoring drowned out by the music.

Ruben Oxworth ambled up to the sofa and said, "Miss Tranquility, I hope you're going to favor us with a melody or two." He directed his next comment to Alex as he added, "She has the sweetest voice. A fellow can get lost in her voice."

"Oh, la, Mr. Oxworth, you'll make me blush."

Alex looked from the young girl at his side up to the weather-worn face of Oxworth. The man was besotted, and he was easily twice her age. There was no accounting for taste.

With a mischievous gleam in his hazel eyes, Alex said, "I look forward to it. If you'll excuse me?" And with this, he made his escape, laughing inwardly at the way Oxworth pounced on the empty space beside Tranquility.

He glanced at Tranquility's face; either she was a very practiced flirt, or she was genuinely pleased with the substitution.

Given a few moments of peace, Alex glanced around the room, observing the knots of people with interest. He watched Chastity glance up, her eyes searching for and finding her mother, and then returning to gaze demurely at her hands folded in her lap. This procedure re-occurred at regular intervals.

He moved a few steps closer, leaning against the cold marble mantel above one of the twin Adam fireplaces. How lonely it must be to be a spinster, treated as a third wheel instead of a favored daughter. His twinge of sympathy was replaced with amusement. The chit wasn't lonely or modest; she was reading. Oh, it would be too bad to let such a prime chance for teasing pass.

He strolled toward the sofa, pretending to look at the paintings on the wall, watching Chastity out of the corner of his eye. As he neared the sofa, she began rearranging her skirts surreptitiously.

Alex slipped into the chair beside her, his knee touching hers. Chastity edged away from him but her movement disturbed the slumbering rector, and he let out a peculiarly loud whistle. Alex stretched out his hand to pluck the book from her lap, but she stood up suddenly, the book falling to the floor with a dull thud.

"Chastity, would you ring for Petrie?" Lady Hartford's voice pierced the air; Alex was surprised by his hostess's agility as she swooped to retrieve the book. She favored her eldest daughter with a particularly withering look.

"Thank you, my lady," said Alex, holding out his hand for the book. "I discovered this book in the library and was asking Miss Chastity if she had read it."

Lady Hartford's pale blue eyes bore into his; then she looked at her daughter, and finally at the volume in her hands. She turned it over to Alex and said sweetly, "I'm sure she has not. My girls do not sully their minds with frivolous novels."

Alex pocketed the book. "Of course not."

"Ring for Petrie, Chastity. It's time for our game." Lady Hartford stood her ground, unwilling to leave Chastity and Alex alone together again.

Chastity did as she was bid, but she favored Alex with a forbidding frown. Moments later, the butler appeared with a porcelain jar, and Lady Hartford began to tap the side with her fan to gain everyone's attention. They gathered closer, Alex standing behind the crowd.

"My dear friends and family, I have thought of the most amusing diversion to entertain the young people. We are going to have a scavenger hunt." There were polite murmurs from her audience. Lady Hartford continued, "I have placed the names of all the young ladies in this jar, and the gentlemen will draw for partners. Miss Bishop's name, of course, has been removed since she will want to have her fiancé Mr. Peaches for her partner."

"What about me, my dear Lady Hartford? I wish to play, too." This from Lady Costain.

"Why, certainly, Lady Costain. And you'll want your husband."

It was difficult to tell who disclaimed first, but both Lord and Lady Costain hastened to protest, Lord Costain saying flatly, "I'm not playing. Margaret can do as she pleases, but count me out."

Lady Hartford's face fell. "Oh, the numbers are uneven. Never mind, Chastity won't mind giving up her place."

Chastity bowed to the inevitable, but her father said, "Nonsense, Divinity! Of course she'll play! One of the other gentlemen will oblige, I'm sure."

Chastity ventured a smile at her father. She did enjoy games of any sort and to have been left out of the scavenger hunt would have rankled.

Lady Hartford eyed her Cousin Virgil, wondering if she could draft him.

Then Ruben Oxworth, her husband's friend, spoke up. "I'll step in, Lady Hartford, if the ladies don't mind the possibility of being partnered by an old bachelor."

The young ladies hurried to reassure him. Lady Costain's name was added to the jar, and Lord Ravenwood stepped up to draw the first name.

"Miss Sincerity," he said happily, moving to stand beside his partner. Sir Charles was next; Lady Hartford waited breathlessly. In her mind, she had singled out Sir Charles as a likely husband for Tranquility. They were both so lively. She threw a venomous look at Lady Costain as Sir Charles called her ladyship's name.

"Mr. Fitzsimmons, you're next," she said sweetly.

Alex looked at Tranquility, who simpered, then at Chastity, who sat quietly awaiting her fate. He took his hand out of his pocket, reached inside the jar, and produced the paper Lord Hartford had given him earlier.

"Miss Chastity."

Her head jerked up; he couldn't tell if she was angry to be selected by him, or alarmed by the purplish tint of her mother's complexion.

"Why, I believe that leaves Miss Tranquility to me," said Ruben Oxworth, his delight showing plainly on his face.

"Mama, tell us what we must find," said Tranquility.

"Yes, Mama, do tell!" echoed Sincerity.

"Very well, I have a list for each of you. Some items are easy to obtain; others, more difficult. But remember, you can't buy any of the items, and you must show them to everyone." She nodded to Petrie, who handed out the lists, one per couple.

Chastity and Alex reached for theirs at the same time. Their hands touched, and they released it simultaneously; it floated to the floor.

"Allow me," said Alex, stooping down and retrieving it.

They read the first line, and Chastity took a step backward. Nervous titters and low rumblings of laughter swept around the room.

"Too daring, Lady Hartford."

Her ladyship giggled and tapped Alex on the arm. "Don't tell me we have a reluctant bachelor, Mr. Fitzsimmons. I expected a blush from the young ladies, but not from you gentlemen," said Lady Hartford.

"With Miss Tranquility's permission," said Ruben. She nodded, and he placed a chaste kiss on her cheek.

Obviously relieved by this proper example, Mr. Peaches followed suit with Miss Bishop. Lord Ravenwood looked rather disappointed, but he, too, delivered a quick touch to Sincerity's cheek.

"Too tame by far for me," said Sir Charles with a leer. Then he proceeded to give Lady Costain a quick kiss, but on the lips instead of the cheek. Everyone laughed at his audacity, including Lord Costain.

"You'd better be careful, Sir Charles, or I'll have to call you out," said his lordship.

All eyes turned to Alex and Chastity. She stiffened. There was no telling with him which example he would follow. Seeing Chastity's trepidation, Alex grinned.

"It's our turn, I suppose, Miss Chastity. Brace yourself." With this, he aimed for her mouth; Chastity scrunched up her face. At the last second, Alex turned slightly and bussed her cheek. Her eyes flew open and met his amused gaze. She wished very much that she could knock him down—not slap him, that was too adult, and he had behaved like a mischievous little boy.

"It wasn't so bad, was it?" he whispered as he turned back to face Lady Hartford, who was already continuing her explanations.

"You are not allowed to buy any of the items, but you may 'borrow' them. One mustn't get caught, however. Whoever has found the most items by Christmas Eve will be declared our winners."

"And what do we win?" asked the undaunted Sir Charles with a wink at his partner.

"That will be revealed at the proper time, Sir Charles. Ah, here's the tea tray. Tranquility, will you pour out, please?" She took a seat beside Lady Ravenwood, Lord Ravenwood's aging grandmother, and leaned over to speak audibly. "One can tell so much about a young lady's breeding by the way she pours out, don't you think?"

Chastity went back to her sofa; Alex followed and sat down by her side, the rector having moved closer to the sweets on the tea tray.

"I hope you're not too upset, Miss Hartford."

"About?" she said airily.

Alex smiled; she was anything but predictable. He had assumed she would want to rip up at him for teasing her about the kiss, but she hadn't.

"Nothing. Shall we study this list?"

"Very well, if we must," said Chastity primly.

"Don't you wish to participate in your mother's scavenger hunt?" he asked.

"Yes, of course I do. We mustn't spoil the game. What's next?"

Alex held out the list.

> One kiss from your partner
> One parrot's feather
> One watchman's lantern
> One crystal snuffbox
> One child's doll
> One skeleton key
> One conch shell
> One whip from a mail coach
> One fisherman's net

"A child's doll! I know where we can find one!" whispered Chastity. "When Tranquility and Sincerity left the nursery, Mother had everything in it thrown out, but I saved one doll that Papa had brought me from Paris. It's hidden in the back of an old chest in the nursery."

Her enthusiasm was contagious, and Alex whispered, "Wonderful! And I happen to know where I can get my hands on a crystal snuffbox. Wait here."

Alex strolled to the door and slipped into the corridor. He reappeared after five minutes and rejoined Chastity. He reached into his pocket and produced a small crystal snuffbox, cupping his large hand so no one would see it.

"Where did it come from?"

Alex grinned. "Charlie."

"Sir Charles?" she said, barely containing her laughter. "But won't he want it?"

"Definitely. That's why we have to hide it till Christmas Eve. We don't want to give it back to him until after the game's up."

Chastity gurgled with laughter. "I thought he was your friend."

"So he is, but all's fair in war and scavenger hunts, and I play to win." He fixed her with a questioning look, and Chastity nodded.

"Me, too," she agreed quietly.

"Good! Now, I want you to take this and find somewhere to hide it. Charlie will know I took it and will search my room."

"I'll find a safe spot. How will we get a mail coach whip?"

Alex's roguish grin beamed forth. "As I see it, we have two choices. We can hide out on the post road and waylay the coach, but that could prove dangerous. I have no desire to be shot for a highwayman. Or we can sneak into the yard of the nearest posting inn and 'borrow' one."

Chastity felt a thrill of excitement coursing through her veins. This was not going to be a dull house party after all. He was being absurd, of course, about their becoming highwaymen. But his daring was evident in the second plan.

"I should be the one to 'borrow' the whip," she whispered, continuing his use of the euphemism.

"You?" he said. "No, I think it would be better for me to take it. You can distract the coachmen and ostlers by swooning."

Chastity drew away and threw back her head, looking down her nose at him. "I never swoon, Mr. Fitzsimmons. You distract them; I'll get the whip."

Alex shook his head, but he was smiling, and agreed. "It's been so long, I'd forgotten how stubborn you are."

"I'll thank you, Mr. Fitzsimmons, not to bring up the past. That little girl no longer exists."

He pretended to be interested in his hand as he said, "Oh, I quite agree, and after kissing the present-day Chastity . . . twice . . . I must say I much prefer the present you."

Chastity stood up and, without a word, left the drawing room, pausing only to bid her mother a quick "good night."

Chapter Two

Alex frowned. Though he wanted Chastity to shun his company, he shouldn't have goaded her in that manner. Even though he had been a callow youth of nineteen on his last visit to his godparents, he had been aware of the depth of Chastity's adoration. He had disdained her; still, she had persisted in following him, never asking for favors. It had been enough for her, at the impressionable age of fourteen or fifteen, to be near him. And he had behaved abominably. In his own defense, Alex recalled, he had been in love with a young lady in the neighborhood. He hadn't set out to flaunt this paragon in Chastity's face, but he had, at that awful picnic. He had seen Chastity watching as they strolled through the garden at sunset, and he had deliberately kissed the young lady at his side. His eyes had met Chastity's, those big, green eyes filling with tears. Then she had turned and fled. He hadn't seen either the young lady or Chastity again.

Until now. He was nine and twenty. He had spent the past four years fighting with Wellesley on the Peninsula. When his assignment here was done, he would return to Spain. There was no time for dalliance, no matter how beautiful those green eyes were, no matter how bewitching that gawky figure of a girl had become.

"A game of billiards, Alex?"

He returned from his reverie and looked up at Sir Charles. He frowned. Charlie had been visiting that summer so many years before. He and Alex had joked about the awkward little girl so head-over-heels in love with Alex. Suddenly, Alex felt a wave of distaste wash over him as he looked up at Charlie. Good old Charlie, still devil-may-care, still supremely self-confident and selfish.

Alex shook his head. "Not tonight, Charlie. Too tired. Think I'll got to bed."

"Suit yourself, old man. Good night. Ravenwood, how about a game of billiards?"

Alex climbed the stairs; he'd been unaware of the passage of time as he'd sat daydreaming. The house was quiet; most of the guests were abed. Chastity, too, of course.

"You, footman. What's your name?"

"William, sir."

"William," began Alex, tossing a coin from one hand to the other. "Where's Miss Chastity's room?"

To his credit, the servant hesitated.

"We're partners in this scavenger hunt, and I want to speak to her—first thing tomorrow morning, of course."

"Ah, well, in that case, Mr. Fitzsimmons, Miss Chastity's in the west hall, third door on the left."

Alex tossed the coin to the footman and strolled away. Then he turned and said, "William."

"Yes, sir."

Alex tossed another coin at the fellow and put one finger to his lips.

"Mum's the word, sir."

When the servant had gone, Alex turned around, making his way to the west corridor. He paused outside the third door on the left. There was a light at the bottom of the door. He lifted his hand to knock.

"You must have done something, Chastity!"

Alex dropped his hand as he recognized Lady Hartford's strident voice. He peered up and down the dark corridor to make certain his presence wasn't being observed. Then he set himself to listening unabashedly.

"How, Mother? I had no idea you'd even planned such an activity."

"Well, you were very cozy on the sofa afterwards."

"We were only talking about the scavenger hunt. If you didn't want me to participate, why did you put my name in the jar?"

"I did that before speaking to Lady Ravenwood. I had no idea Sir Charles's pockets were to let when I invited him. And that has left only young Ravenwood and Mr. Fitzsimmons for the girls. Still, even with no fortune, I prefer Sir Charles to Ruben Oxworth for Tranquility. Oh, I don't know! Everything has gone wrong!"

"I'm sorry, Mother," said Chastity. Alex could hear the weariness in her voice.

Her mother sighed. "Ah, well, I suppose we'll come about. But you must remember, Mr. Fitzsimmons is for Tranquility. You can help by telling him all about her."

"Yes, Mother."

"Now, get some sleep."

Alex hurried down the hall and around the corner, out of sight. He remained there until he heard a second door close. He had started back down the hall when Chastity's door opened again, and she stepped into the corridor carrying a candle. Silently, he followed her.

Chastity stopped at the foot of the back stairs and listened. All was quiet, and she mounted the stairs, making her way toward the old nursery. She entered the schoolroom, which had become a storage area since her sisters' last governess had been dismissed.

There, in the corner, was the old green cupboard. Unmindful of the dust, Chastity pushed chairs and tables aside and crossed the room. She almost had to crawl into the cupboard to retrieve the forgotten doll.

"Is it there?"

"Ouch!" Chastity straightened up and glared at Alex. "What are you doing here? Following me?"

Alex chuckled. "Are you all right? Didn't mean to frighten you. Did you bump your head?"

"Yes, I bumped my head," grumbled Chastity. "Don't tell me you got lost on your way to bed."

"And came looking for you for assistance?" he asked dryly. "No, but I did take a wrong turn, which is why I happened to see this mysterious figure creeping stealthily down the hall and up the back stairs. I thought we had robbers."

"Very well, I acquit you of setting out deliberately to molest me."

"Good! Now, is it there?"

"Yes," she said, pulling out a parcel wrapped in dusty tissue. "I just wanted to be certain. I'll put the snuffbox with it."

"You can't do that. You'll have to find a new hiding place for both of them."

"Why? No one would ever think to come in here."

Alex shook his head and reached down to help Chastity rise. She was looking particularly lovely in her wrapper, with her hair falling around her shoulders. He reminded himself to stick to business and continued, "Not as a rule, but this scavenger hunt will have people searching all over this house for the items on the list. And one look in this room, the footprints in the dusty floor, the handprints on the cupboard. . ."

"You're right, of course. I hadn't thought."

"You'd better take the doll and snuffbox to your room for tonight. We'll find somewhere else to hide them tomorrow. Some place outside the house."

"You've got a very suspicious mind, Mr. Fitzsimmons.

Most people wouldn't reason things out like you did," she said, stepping past him.

"I don't know whether to say thank you or not. Why don't you call me Alex, Chastity?"

She looked him directly in the eyes. He was very close, his breath ruffling the tendrils of hair around her face. There had been a time when Alex Fitzsimmons's proximity would have sent her into a fit of the vapors. Now, other than a certain shyness, she felt nothing—no tingling, no vapors.

He took her hand, and Chastity steeled herself against his touch. But nothing happened; her knees didn't even go weak.

"Won't you?" he asked again.

Chastity retrieved her hand and said candidly, "Not tonight. Not here. Perhaps tomorrow, Mr. Fitzsimmons."

She left him then, and Alex remained where he was, bemused by her composure. She was not the young girl he remembered. And he rather liked her this way.

His ruminations were interrupted by the realization that he could see lights through the nursery window. He'd never thought about it before, but the Hartford's house faced the Channel, although it was set a mile or so back from the shore and there were woods between the water and the house. But from up there on the third floor, he could see the sea. Or could he? All he could really see were two faint lights, shuttered and opened three times. Then they were gone. A signal?

It was hard to judge the distance. Perhaps they came from the woods. Possibly it was someone poaching rabbits in the home wood.

Alex remained by the window for some time before finally giving up. He would investigate the next day to see if there was any evidence of poachers in the woods. And if the day was clear, he would climb back up to the third floor to judge the source of the lights. With his thumb, he marked their position on the dirty glass of the window. Tomorrow, he would see.

The morning brought fog, though it remained unseasonably warm. Alex restrained his frustration, picked up his cane, and set out for the woods. He turned at the edge of the trees, his keen eyes searching the shrouded facade of the stone house for the schoolroom window. With the fog, it was impossible to judge if the lights had come from where he was now standing.

The ground was moist with dew, and his boots were soon sodden. Although he carried his cane, he twirled it around rather than making use of it. His gait was sure and steady with no trace of a limp.

Half an hour later, Alex left the thinning trees and found himself looking across a wide expanse of scrubby sand to the English Channel. The fog was burning off, but the gray water looked cold and uninviting.

"Buster! Come here, you silly dog!"

Alex stepped back into the shelter of the trees and watched as Chastity clapped her hands and shouted again for the recalcitrant hound. Alex saw the dog heading his way and stepped forward, walking toward Chastity with a pronounced limp.

"Good morning!" he said cheerily.

She erased the fleeting frown and smiled at him. Or was it at her dog? Alex thought wryly.

"What are you doing out here? Most of the guests are still asleep," Chastity asked, unable to disguise her displeasure.

"Probably, but I remembered how pleasant an early morning stroll on the beach can be. Are you in the habit of rising so early?"

She gave him a smile of genuine amusement. "Surely, for a soldier, ten o'clock seems rather late."

"Sleeping till all hours is a habit I can easily slip back into," he commented, petting the dog. "But you didn't answer my question," he added as they fell in step beside each other.

"Yes, I find morning the best part of the day. I can do as I please without anyone telling me I shouldn't." She glanced at him defiantly.

His voice was gentle as he said, "How can anyone object to your taking a walk with your dog?"

Chastity smiled and said, "Now do wear a hat! And make sure you don't get the hem of your gown wet, and do take a footman!"

"And don't forget, 'you'll catch your death of cold, young man!' "

She laughed at his high-pitched mimicry, but her amusement faded quickly, leaving a touch of envy. "But you, Alex, you get to grow up, leave home, do as you please every day."

"Fight in a war," he added.

"True. And I don't mean to belittle how gruesome that must be. But to me, it seems like freedom. Only girls aren't allowed to want to wander. They are supposed to marry and stay home and have babies." She blanched as she realized how intimate their conversation had become. Her mother would be apoplectic if she overheard such a conversation!

"I'd never thought of that," said Alex, stopping and looking her in the eye. "But you mustn't romanticize a man's life, Chastity. There are duties and responsibilities aplenty."

"I know, I know. I just wish sometime I could be my own master—or rather, mistress." She decided to change the subject.

She had been on the verge of telling him her dream,

her plan for escape. He would have laughed; he would have called it ridiculous. He wasn't really interested in her opinions; he was just being polite.

"What shall we look for today?" she asked, as she continued along.

"I had hoped we might find the seashell on the beach."

"They are so rare here. There's a cave down the beach. When the tide is high, the water covers the floor of the cave. We might find one there."

"I wonder . . ." Alex took out his timepiece. "It's almost eleven o'clock. We should be getting back. It's too bad my godfather's not still alive. He had a huge collection of shells from his visits to the West Indies."

"I remember that. As a child, when I would visit at your godparents', your godfather would tell me all about his collection of shells. I loved listening to the sea."

"I wonder what happened to them," said Alex.

"Do you suppose they might still be in the house? Didn't he keep them in that tiny study behind the library?"

"Right, but surely his heirs took them. If not, the present owner probably threw them away."

"We could ride over this afternoon and ask. I am somewhat acquainted with the comtesse; I'm sure she wouldn't mind if we looked for them," said Chastity.

"Good idea. Only let's take my curricle. I'm not up to riding yet."

"Oh! I wasn't thinking. Of course we'll take the curricle. Do you want me to drive?"

Alex stopped in his tracks, frowning fiercely down at her, his height making her feel small despite her stature.

"I will drive, thank you. I'm not a complete invalid. And the only other person I trust with my grays is my tiger."

"I'm a competent whip," said Chastity.

"It takes more than competence to drive my cattle," he said, setting off across the sand at a snappy pace.

Chastity watched him for a moment, her indignation cooling before a frown wrinkled her brow. Where was his limp?

Suddenly, as if Alex had read her mind, the limp reappeared. She was puzzled; why would anyone pretend to be injured? What could he hope to gain? Sympathy? She shook her head. That was absurd. From what she had seen of Alex Fitzsimmons, he would never find sympathy pleasing. Perhaps he only limped when he was tired. She tried to remember if he had depended on his cane the day before. She hadn't noticed.

"Alex! Wait for me!" she called.

He stopped and turned to grin at her, leaning heavily on the cane as if to emphasize his dependence on it.

"Then hurry up, Chastity!"

Alex waited impatiently by his curricle for Chastity to appear. His grays stamped their hoofs, reflecting their eagerness to be gone.

He was looking forward to meeting the Frenchwoman. It seemed too great a coincidence that her appearance coincided with the increase in spy activity along this section of the coast.

It was a nerve-wracking time for people in Sussex. Here, where you could stand on the cliffs of Dover and see France on a clear day, everyone was readying for Napoleon's invasion of England. There were towers of wood for bonfires along the entire coast, with watchmen ready to set them ablaze on the first sign of a French invasion. Despite these preparations, they remained vulnerable. The fact of the matter was that there were not half enough troops to be roused. The bonfires would be the signals, but there was no army standing ready to defend the coast.

And that was all the more reason that he should discover the traitor or traitors who were smuggling French spies into the country. If these spies related to Napoleon just how weak their defenses were . . .

"Alex, are you ready?" Chastity asked for the second time.

"What? Yes, I . . . You look beautiful," he finished, surprising himself as well as Chastity.

"Thank you," she said, hoping the comtesse would respond as Alex had. She was wearing a forest-green velvet carriage dress. It was one of her favorites, though her mother deemed it dull and unattractive. She felt it was one of her most sophisticated gowns, and she wanted to look her most fashionable when she visited the comtesse. The woman had a way of looking down her nose at one; it never failed to make Chastity feel dowdy.

Alex, on the other hand, was flattered that she had set out to look her best for him. This feeling quickly changed to uneasiness. He had assumed Chastity would be easier to work with than her sisters. He hoped she wouldn't prove him wrong by falling in love with him or trying to set up a flirtation with him.

"Watch the gate," warned Chastity as they wheeled past the gatekeeper's cottage and into the lane.

"I can manage, thank you. Just hold on tight if you're afraid."

Chastity folded her arms across her chest and stared straight ahead. Alex glanced at her and with an expert flick of his whip, sent the horses careening down the road at an alarming rate, causing Chastity to clutch the seat. He grinned and pulled back slightly on the ribbons.

They turned into the neglected drive and a slovenly gatekeeper came out of his dilapidated house and growled, "What do you want?" in a heavy French accent.

"We want to see your mistress," said Alex.

With a grunt that could have passed for a laugh, he waved them through.

Alex shook his head dolefully as they progressed up the drive. There were deep ruts, and it was overgrown with grass. Broken-down fences lined the drive, and where once sheep had grazed, only weeds grew.

"I can't believe how bad it is. It hasn't been that many years since I last visited."

"True, but for five years the house stood empty. The comtesse says she is trying to bring it back to its former state."

They arrived at the front steps. No groom or footman appeared to take their horses. The house looked unoccupied except for one open window.

"Some improvement, eh?" Alex leapt down and turned to help Chastity. He grasped her waist, swinging her easily to the ground. "I wonder if we'll have to let ourselves in," he said, staring up the steps. The door, which should have swung open upon their arrival, remained shut tight. The well-manicured lawn was a forgotten memory. The estate, it seemed, was no better off since the arrival of its new mistress. And there was no sign of servants or workmen setting things to rights.

They climbed the steps after Alex secured the team to the newel post, grumbling all the while about keeping his cattle standing. He lifted the heavy knocker, and it sounded loudly.

After several minutes, the door swung open and a tiny, grizzled man asked. *"Qu'est-ce que vous voulez?* What ees it you want?"

"Votre maitresse, elle est ici?"

"Oui, she ees here. Come with me, please." The dwarf turned and led them down the dark hallway. Dark,

thought Chastity, because the leaded glass panes around the tall front doors were dirty and dingy.

The room they entered was surprisingly bright and clean. Alex noted that it was the one room whose windows were open. A thin, dark-haired woman rose as they entered.

"How do you do, Miss Hartford? It's so good of you to call," said the woman with a French accent.

Chastity dipped a quick curtsey. "Thank you for seeing me, Comtesse. Allow me to present Mr. Alexander Fitzsimmons."

"Enchanté, comtesse," said Alex with a gallant bow.

"Alexander," she said slowly, allowing the name to roll gently from her lips. "A charming name for a handsome man. Won't you be seated?" She turned and snapped her fingers. The butler toddled forward, and she gave him instructions.

"How are you settling in? Do you like Folkestone?" asked Chastity.

"Oh, it is losing its strangeness. But it is very slow, putting the house in order. I have tried hiring girls from the village, but they think my dear Jean-Jacques is too strange. They are frightened of him. So, I must do with my cook, Jean-Jacques, and my gatekeeper, Remi.

"It must be very difficult for you, living in a strange land," said Alex in perfect French.

"Oh, *oui,* but it is much to be preferred over *la guillotine,"* said the comtesse smoothly.

"True. Did you lose your family?" asked Alex.

The comtesse dabbed her eyes with a lacy handkerchief. Alex wondered why; there didn't appear to be any tears.

"My dear husband, the comte. He made me leave without him. I was in hiding for a year before I escaped to England. It is painful to recall."

"I'm sorry, comtesse; we didn't mean to distress you," said Chastity, throwing a reproachful look at Alex.

"Thank you. Ah, here is the tea tray. You see, I have adopted some of your ways, although I prefer wine, myself."

"Wine would be fine with me," said Alex, and the comtesse handed him a glass.

"I'm afraid my cook has not mastered the art of your biscuits. But I see he has offered some tarts and pastries. Mademoiselle?"

"Thank you," said Chastity, accepting a cup of tea and an apple tart.

They partook of the refreshments, and Chastity was trying to think of a way to broach the topic of the seashells when the comtesse spoke.

"But I think you came here to ask me for something, eh?" Chastity and Alex exchanged glances. "Otherwise, you would have waited until tomorrow evening when your charming mother has invited me to your ball."

"As a matter of fact, we do have a favor to ask. Mr. Fitzsimmons is the godson of the people who used to live here," began Chastity.

"This is so? Then you wish to see the house—for old-time's sake, I believe is the expression."

"That is the expression, comtesse, but that is not why we are here. Another time, perhaps. Miss Hartford and I have teamed up on a scavenger hunt."

"Scavenger hunt?" she asked.

"It's a game where you are given a list of items and a certain length of time, and you try to find all the things on the list."

"Oh, I see. How may I help you?"

"My godfather had a collection of seashells, and we need one for the hunt."

"He kept them in a back room behind his study."

"I am familiar with this room," said the comtesse.

With a Gallic shrug, she added, "But it is empty. I have, however, a seashell that I will lend you. I found it when I went to the Cote d'Azur, in the south of France. Have you ever been there, monsieur?"

Alex shook his head. "I have seen the Mediterranean, but from the coast of Spain."

"When you were a boy?"

"No, not long ago." Was it his imagination, or did the comtesse stiffen? With her next words, he decided he must have been mistaken.

"You must have been in the army fighting that awful Napoleon!" she said vehemently.

"Yes, until I was injured. Now, I'm home for good," he said, tapping his cane beside the chair.

"Well, I am glad. I do not want Napoleon to succeed, *naturellement*, but I am glad to know you, a handsome young man, won't be killed by a Frenchman's musket."

Chastity didn't approve of the leer with which this speech was delivered, and she said hastily, "The seashell, comtesse, may we see it?"

"Of course, *chérie*, I will go and find it at once." With a lingering glance in Alex's direction, the Fenchwoman left them alone.

"Well, that was certainly unpleasant," said Chastity.

"What?" said Alex with innocent eyes.

"The way she fawned all over you."

"I didn't mind," he said innocently.

"I daresay."

"She is rather attractive, in a gypsy-ish sort of way. Rather exotic," Alex added.

Chastity sniffed audibly. "She must be all of forty."

"True, but older women . . ."

Chastity glared at him and concentrated on getting down the strong, tepid tea in her cup. Obviously the French chef had not yet mastered the art of making tea either.

"No need to get all puffed up."

She peered at him over the rim of her cup, set it down deliberately, and turned her back on him.

Alex just grinned and stood up. Moving around the room, he picked up several ceramic knick-knacks, pretending a great interest in them. He went to the open window and stared outside. His curricle had disappeared, claimed, he supposed, by the comtesse's servant.

"What do you think of her, Chastity?" he asked quietly.

"Think of her? You mean do I think she would be willing to be your mistress?" asked Chastity tartly, throwing good manners and caution to the wind. So what if Alex Fitzsimmons developed a disgust for her!

Alex laughed and moved behind the sofa where Chastity was sitting, causing her to swivel around to watch his restless movements. "No, I mean, your opinion. What feeling do you get about her?"

Chastity had no idea why he would ask her such a question, but she decided to answer him anyway. "She makes me uncomfortable. I can't say why."

"Perhaps because she is French?"

"No, I don't think so. I had a very good friend at school who was French. I am accustomed to their ways."

"Hmm."

"What do you think?" countered Chastity.

They heard footsteps in the hall, and he leaned over the back of the sofa and whispered in her ear, "I think she is returning."

When they arrived back at Hartford House, Alex dropped Chastity off at the front door with their borrowed seashell safely stowed in her reticule. He took the team around to the stable yard and gave them up to his tiger.

With cane in hand, he walked along the row of stalls, peering into each one. The head groomsman paused in his work as Alex stood looking across a paddock where a huge gray stallion was grazing.

"We have to keep him separate from th' others, so he's got his own stall in his own paddock. He's the fastest 'orse in th' stable, guvner."

"Oh? Lord Hartford's horse?" asked Alex, moving over to the fence. The big horse came closer, taking the carrot Alex had pulled out of his pocket.

"Lud, no. Belongs t' Miss Chastity, 'e does," said Hale, joining Alex.

"Hmm. So she likes to ride neck or nothing."

"That's a fact, guvner. 'Course," he added, rubbing the white blaze on the stallion's face, "'e's as gentle as a lamb. Unusual in a stud, but there you are. Miss Chastity raised 'im that way. She calls 'im Baby."

"Does she allow anyone else to ride him?"

"Nobody. That's th' only time 'e turns nasty is when someun else gets on 'is back."

"I'll try and remember that." Alex slipped another carrot to the big horse and moved on.

"Let me look at all of you," said Lady Hartford. Her daughters lined up obediently. "I knew that shade of pink would brighten up those cheeks," she said to Sincerity. "And Tranquility, you look charming in the green."

"Thank you, Mama."

"Chastity . . ." Her mother walked around her, eyeing the yellow gown with a puzzled expression. "I don't remember that dress."

"It's rather old," Chastity said, hoping her mother

wouldn't recall their last conversation about this particular dress. It had been selected by her mother during
her one Season in London. It was outmoded now, not
having the latest raised waistline, but Chastity thought it
would do. At the time it was made, however, Chastity
had complained about the low-cut bodice and refused to
wear it, angering her mother. But now, tonight, she felt
the need of something different, and for her, the
scooped neckline that showed her cleavage was daring.

"It would be better if it had a higher waistline. It is
terribly outmoded," said Lady Hartford, oblivious to her
daughter's feelings or the fact that it hugged Chastity's
tiny waist and showed off her well-developed bust.

"I think it's lovely," said Tranquility. "And Chastity
looks beautiful in that particular shade of yellow. Now,
I could not wear it, with my hair."

"True," said Sincerity, "but with her brown hair, it is
most becoming."

"Yes, yes, I suppose you're right. Very well, girls, let's
go downstairs. And remember, be on your best behavior."

"Yes, Mama."

"Now, you girls run along. Chastity, I want to speak
to you a moment."

Chastity waited, her face masked. What had she done
now?

"Have you been telling Fitzsimmons about Tranquility? I know you've spent today in his company. I hope
you're not putting yourself forward."

"No, Mother."

"Oh, how I wish Fitzsimmons had picked Tranquility's name! You would have dealt much better with
Oxworth."

"I'm sorry, Mother," said Chastity automatically.

"Well, we must make the best of it!" said Lady Hartford briskly. "I know you'll do your best for Tranquility.

He'll be seated beside her at dinner, of course, so they can have some time together."

"Of course," said Chastity, echoing her mother in a small voice.

Dinner was a congenial affair, less formal than the previous evening, the various guests having become more accustomed to each other and their surroundings. Chastity had to admit that her mother had been right about the scavenger hunt providing a topic of conversation. Lady Costain, seated beside Sir Charles, was monopolizing all his time; Sincerity and Lord Ravenwood whispered and giggled secretively.

Chastity now had Mr. Peaches on one side while Cousin Virgil remained on the other, so she was left in peace, both gentlemen paying particular attention to their other dinner companions. She was not dismayed by this since she enjoyed the company of her own thoughts.

After dinner, the party split up, some choosing cards while two or three couples took their places on a makeshift dance floor, and Chastity played the pianoforte.

The light airs required by the dancers were so familiar to her, that she was able to let her mind wander. The date was December 18; six months from this day, she would be five and twenty. More importantly, she would come into her inheritance—a mere pittance by the *Ton's* standards, but enough annually to support the modest lifestyle she had planned. This time, next Christmas, she would be her own mistress, somewhere.

"Play another one, Chastity," said Sincerity, startling her back to the present.

As she shuffled through sheafs of music, Tranquility taunted, "Chastity is so distracted, she must be thinking of a beau."

Chastity turned a bright red, looking over the piano-forte to where the card players had paused in their play to stare at her. She knew her color proclaimed her guilt, and she wanted to protest, to berate her sister, but she was speechless.

"Perhaps," said Alex, his chair scraping the floor as he pushed back from the card table, "Miss Chastity is merely wishing someone else would take her turn at the instrument so she might dance." He directed a pointed stare at Tranquility, who set her jaw mulishly.

Sincerity held back a moment, then laughed and said, "Well, I should think so. I'll play, Chastity; I love to play!"

Kindly, Chastity did not point out that Sincerity hated playing the pianoforte. Instead, she simply thanked her sister and tried to circumvent Alex to gain the sofa at the far end of the room, but he would have none of it.

"May I have this dance?"

"But you would be leaving your table short one player," she protested.

"I'm sure Sir Charles will take my place," he said, signaling his friend. "Won't you, old man?" It was not a request.

"My pleasure, though I expect to have my turn with Miss Chastity, too." The look he bestowed on her approached a leer, and Chastity took a step backward. Alex frowned fiercely at his friend before offering his arm to Chastity.

"But what about your leg?" Chastity said desperately.

Alex brushed this aside, saying he could certainly limp through one dance.

The dance was a country reel, the steps easy to follow, and the separations curtailing any chance of intimate conversation. On the whole, Chastity found the experience refreshing. She purposely refused to meet her mother's eye.

When that set was over, a second followed, and she was partnered by a sulky Lord Ravenwood who kept eyeing Sincerity's back and sighing vociferously. As the set ended, Chastity looked up to find her mother's wicked brow arched dangerously.

"I'll take over again, Sincerity," she said to her sister, and Sincerity was on her feet in a flash, one hand snaking around Lord Ravenwood's arm while she tapped Sir Charles, who had returned to the dancers, playfully on the arm. Chastity took her place at the instrument.

"Another time, Miss Chastity," Sir Charles said quietly in her ear as he leaned over her, ostensibly looking at the music.

Chastity shrank from him as he laid one familiar hand on her shoulder before turning to select another partner.

Victim, rather, Chastity thought to herself. Why was he behaving so? A flash of realization crossed her features, and it was all she could do to continue playing. Sir Charles knew about her past—somehow. He had heard the old rumors and was behaving accordingly. She looked across the room at her mother. No, she decided, her mother would not be so indiscreet. Then her frightening gaze fell on Lady Costain, who delivered a malicious smile and said something in Sir Charles's ear.

Chastity's blush faded; her face became white with anger. How could anyone be so cruel? Exerting amazing self-control, Chastity plowed through the tune without a mistake. She played another and another. By the time the guests began to tire, she had regained her composure; she bade everyone good night and slipped away.

When I retire from society completely, I might just change my name, Chastity decided as she pulled up the covers. I certainly never want to see any of these people again! There! On that thought, I can sleep peacefully.

But Chastity was not so lucky. Lady Costain's maliciousness was too upsetting. With a weary sigh, she relighted the candles and picked up a romance novel she had ordered from London—her one extravagance.

"How about it, Alex? A game of billiards? Ravenwood was too easy; I need a little more of a challenge," said Sir Charles.

Alex laughed. "Very well, I'll play." He had planned to go out, but it was only midnight, and he still had an hour or two before the house was quiet. They were alone in the spacious game room, so called because its shelves were lined with games of all sorts—ornate chess and backgammon sets, an ancient board game from India called Shaturanga, and another called Hala-tafl, a pre-runner of the popular game Fox and Geese. In the center of the room was a heavily carved billiard table.

"You're a sly one, Alex," said Sir Charles, breaking expertly.

"How so?" asked Alex, leaning against the wall nonchalantly. Had he slipped up somehow? Did Charles guess his true reason for being at Hartford House? Not that Charles was suspect, of course.

Charles's chuckle was wicked, knowing. "Miss Chastity. Quite a triumph drawing her for your partner."

Alex frowned, perplexed. Cautiously, he agreed and added, "She's very clever. Up to every rig and row. You don't stand a chance."

Charlie looked up from the table and his merry eyes met Alex's. "Is that a challenge, old man?"

"You know I play to win," said Alex, not catching his friend's double-entendre.

"Always, but I think the lady has some say in this.

Not that she's that choosy. I understand it was Winchester the first time. What a waste!"

Alex placed his cue stick on the table, moving several of the colorful balls as he did.

"What are you talking about, Charlie?"

Sir Charles's wicked grin disappeared, and he leaned closer with glee. "Do you mean you honestly don't know?"

"Stow it, Charlie. What are you talking about?"

Sir Charles ignored his friend's growing anger and rocked on his heels thoughtfully. "This has a number of interesting possibilities. I mean, I could just savor her myself."

"What the hell!" Alex grabbed his friend's lapels and straightened his stance roughly.

"No, it really would be too shameful to keep it to myself," said Sir Charles, gently removing Alex's hands, looking around the empty room, and then indicating two chairs.

"I had the story from Lady Costain. Doesn't it puzzle you that a young lady as beautiful as Chastity Hartford should be unmarried, secluded here in this God-forsaken corner of the country?" He paused, but shrugged and continued at Alex's fierce growl. "Well, the reason is she ruined herself during her first Season. With Winchester, of all people. Why, he couldn't have been more than twenty at the time. There was a big scandal. He had to offer for her, but she refused. Made her mother furious, as you can well imagine. So she's been buried here ever since, yearning for a second chance at, uh, male companionship."

Alex sat back, astounded. It made sense. Why hadn't she married? She was beautiful and witty, and . . .

"Rich, isn't it, with a name like Chastity! The gossips had a field day with that!"

Chastity, ruined. He recalled that brief kiss under the

mistletoe and frowned again. She hadn't behaved like a demimonde. Why, she had been shocked.

"Rubbish!" he announced firmly. "Anyone can see she's everything decent and proper."

"Ah, the quiet ones . . ."

"Rubbish!" Alex said again. "And if you so much as look at her wrong, Charlie, I'll draw your cork."

"If you think you can," said his friend bravely as he rose.

Alex stood up, too, and said confidently, "You know I can."

Sir Charles grimaced but nodded his agreement.

"Good! Now, how about that game?"

Alex had no trouble with the stallion; he'd always had a way with horses. He tethered Baby to a bush at the edge of the tree line and raised a spyglass to his eye, his gaze carefully following the beach. He needed to get closer, but the sky was clear and the quarter moon lighted the marshy stretch of downs that led to the beach.

After two hours of cramped muscles, he gave up and returned to the house, rubbing the stallion down with straw and closing the paddock gate. Anyone involved in secretive comings and goings on the coast would wait for a darker night.

Chastity watched with a frown as the shadowy figure of a man crossed the garden and short span of open lawn to the house, disappearing from view. Had she imagined it? She looked back at the novel about dark castles and ghostly presences and smiled. It was time she put the book aside and went to sleep.

* * *

The next day, Chastity slept late, waking only when the sun became too bright. She went to the windows, her thoughts briefly taken up with wondering about the man she had seen outside the previous night. She shrugged; it had probably only been the novel and the lateness of the hour. Thinking of the book, she crawled back into bed, picked it up, and began to read.

After a moment, Chastity set it aside with a sigh. Nothing was ever that good, that perfect. She dressed and went downstairs, wanting to take a walk in the warm afternoon sun. She went through the kitchens, grinned at the cook, and grabbed an apple from the bowl.

"That's for my tart!" protested the cook sternly.

"It's only one, Cookie," she pleaded.

"Oh, go on with you, do!"

Chastity sat down and started paring the apple. "How is your daughter?"

"She's fine; tired of waiting for the baby."

"And James?"

"Th' lad tries, but he's not very patient. And he wants to give her everything on a silver platter. Treats her like a princess."

"He's not . . ."

"No, he swears he's given it up for good."

"I hope he has. It's entirely too dangerous. Do you think they would like a Christmas basket? It could come from me and you. You can pack some of your wonderful tarts . . ."

"That would be nice, Miss Chastity. James is proud, but I think it would be acceptable if it came from the two of us. That's not charity, is it?"

"Certainly not! Just a gift for friends," said Chastity. "We'll make it up and I'll take it over first thing in the morning."

"Chastity, what are you doing down here? I just sent your sisters to bed," chided her mother, taking the apple and placing it on the table.

"But I'm not slee . . ."

"But you will be at the ball tonight if you don't get some sleep! Now, get to bed!"

"But, Mother—" she protested.

Her mother lifted her nose in the air and peered up at Chastity for a moment.

"Yes, Mother," said Chastity, throwing a look of appeal toward the cook.

Cook winked and nodded.

Chastity started up the stairs, passing Alex on the way. He was dressed for hunting.

"Where are you going?" she asked wistfully.

He glanced down at his tweed jacket and buckskin trousers and said, "Hunting, I should think. Want to come along?" He grinned.

Chastity looked down the long staircase and saw her mother's keen eyes on her.

"No, thank you, Mr. Fitzsimmons. I must get my rest before the big ball tonight."

Alex had seen his hostess's interested gaze and nodded. "Good day, then," he said, sketching a quick bow before continuing on his way.

Chastity trudged reluctantly to her room, grumbling mentally. If she'd only been born a boy, she, too, could be off on a jaunt through the woods. But no, she was constrained to go to her room and rest! And she'd only just left it!

She went to the window and watched Alex, accompanied by the gamekeeper, stride across the green lawns and disappear into the woods.

With gritted teeth, Chastity turned and went to the bed. Everyone knew she never pulled all the bed curtains closed, but she pulled one side as though trying to shut out the sun. Next, she arranged pillows in a line, and covered them with the counterpane, fluffing here and tucking there. She stood back and scrutinized her work. She nodded, satisfied. Finally, she removed her shoes, put them beside the bed, and took out her half boots.

Easing the door open, Chastity glanced in both directions and hurried down the hall to the back stairs. She peeked cautiously into the kitchen.

Cook put one finger in her mouth and cocked her head toward the larder. With a move surprisingly swift for one of Cook's size, she handed Chastity a small bundle, tied up by a napkin. Chastity blew her a kiss and backed out of the kitchen, making her way to another of the servants' exits.

She skirted the kitchen garden and gave a soft whistle. Buster trotted forward eagerly, and they were shortly out of sight of the house.

In the shade of the trees, it was considerably cooler and Chastity found herself wishing she had thought to bring a cape or shawl. She sat down on a fallen tree and proceeded to share the contents of her napkin with the dog. He was particularly pleased by the chicken bone she gave him. A fresh scone, the apple, and a sweetmeat finished her luncheon.

The crack of a fowling piece reminded Chastity that there were hunters in the wood, and she decided it would be best to go to the beach. Buster, however, had other ideas.

He, too, had heard the report of the gun, and he set off in that direction, his nose to the ground. Chastity whistled, but he refused to respond.

"Wretched dog," she muttered as she set out in pursuit.

When she next set eyes on Buster, he was sitting obe

diently at the feet of Alex, looking from his mistress back to his chosen master with adoration.

"Buster! You naughty dog! You could have been hurt!" she scolded.

Alex laughed and handed his fowling piece to Murphy, the gamekeeper.

"That's all for today, I should think."

"Right you are, Mr. Fitzsimmons." He nodded to Chastity, replaced his hat, and headed back to the house.

"You needn't stop hunting because of me, Mr. Fitzsimmons," said Chastity.

"Not you—or not just you." He reached down and stroked the glossy head at his knee, his actions bonding him to the dog irrevocably. "Buster, here, doesn't quite understand how to be a hunting dog. He thinks running helter-skelter through the woods should suffice."

Chastity smiled. "I'm afraid I never taught him how to hunt."

"Never mind that. He's an obedient little thing."

"For you, perhaps," said Chastity, bending down and patting Buster's head.

"I've always had a way with animals," said Alex quietly.

Chastity straightened up and found herself gazing directly into intense hazel eyes. She shivered.

"You're cold. Take my jacket." As Alex removed his coat, Chastity watched in fascination, taking in the snowy shirtsleeves that revealed strong, muscular arms. Alex placed the tweed jacket around her shoulders, and she shivered again.

He began to rub her arms; the fabric and friction warmed her, and Chastity took a step back.

"Maybe we should get you home. You could catch a chill."

"I'm fine," she protested, not wanting to return to the confines of the house. "Let's walk to the beach."

"If you're sure. I don't want to lose my scavenger hunt partner to a bout of the ague."

"I'm sure," she said, and began walking through the woods toward the beach.

Alex looked down at Buster, shrugged, and followed. "Come along, old boy."

They walked in silence until they reached the beach. The sun was out, making it seem quite warm. Chastity shrugged out of the jacket and returned it to Alex. She leaned down, picked up a stick, and threw it. Buster scampered after it.

"I see you're not using your cane today," said Chastity, walking in the direction she had thrown the stick.

"No, my leg's better, I think. Must be the sea air."

Alex swung the jacket over his shoulder and fell into step beside Chastity. "What will your mother do if she finds you've escaped?"

"She'll read me a lecture."

"She won't forbid you to attend the ball?" Alex asked, a note of alarm creeping into his tone.

"Of course not; I am much too useful in such situations. Besides, there might be questions, and Mother hates to lie. She'd have to tell everyone how disobedient I had been."

Alex shook his head. "You remember what we talked about the other day?" Chastity frowned and looked at him questioningly. "Freedom, remember?" She nodded. "Well, I've changed my mind. I think having the responsibilities of managing an estate, even going to war, are preferable to being always under someone else's control."

Chastity stopped and looked up at him. At that moment, gazing into those hazel eyes fringed with long, black lashes, she understood why she had fallen head over heels in love at the tender age of fourteen. He was more than handsome; he was sympathetic; he listened.

Alex raised a brow, bemused by her manner, her silence.

"Thank you," Chastity said quietly.

Alex let the jacket fall to the sand and took her hand in both of his.

"Woof! Woof!" They turned and saw Buster drop the stick he had fetched, wag his tail, pick it up, then drop it, and wag his tail again.

Chastity removed her hand and started toward the foxhound. He grabbed the stick and ran off a few paces.

"Buster, you naughty thing! Give me the stick!"

The dog edged forward and dropped it. Chastity took a step, and again he grabbed the stick, backing away, teasing her.

"Buster!" she said fiercely, and started after him.

Alex laughed and sat down on the jacket, prepared to enjoy the show.

Chastity returned a few minutes later, sans dog, sans stick, her cheeks glowing, her chest rising and falling rapidly as she tried to catch her breath. Alex moved off the jacket and patted it. Chastity joined him.

They sat in silence for some time, gazing at the sea.

It grew awkward, or so Chastity thought, her hand by her side, so close to his.

"Tell me about Spain," she said, her voice startling some nearby seagulls into flight.

"What would you like to know? The landscape? The towns? Before or after the two armies finished with them?" His voice was matter-of-fact.

"I'm sorry, Alex. I suppose it did sound rather callous." And then she did it; she touched his arm.

Alex turned to face her. Her innocent question had brought back a sudden flood of memories, of men cry-ing out in pain and the silence of the dead. He wanted to pull her to him roughly, to shut it all out with passion.

But he looked into those green eyes, filled with sympathy. He couldn't use her thus. She was too open, too naive. Alex took a deep breath and leaned forward, his lips brushing hers.

Sympathy fled from those beautiful eyes, replaced by . . . Was it fear?

Chastity shook her head and clambered to her feet; catching the hem of her gown under one shoe, she almost fell. Alex, also standing now, caught her. She tore herself free and began to walk rapidly, almost running from the beach.

"Chastity! Wait! I'm sorry." he called. He watched her shake her head adamantly, but she never slowed her pace.

Chastity was thankful Alex hadn't caught her up. She couldn't have faced him. Why were men like that? And how could he know about her?

She reached the woods and stopped, glancing over her shoulder. Alex was lagging far behind, Buster trotting at his heels.

She wanted to cry out, but she didn't. Instead, she turned on her heel and headed back to the house at a brisk pace.

Chastity could feel the humiliation ebb and flow. It was like being back in London. The realization of what could happen to one's reputation had hit her hard then. It was followed fast by anger when she was made to understand that all her shame and troubles would be at an end when she married Lord Winchester.

She had protested that she didn't love Lord Winchester, didn't even like him that much. To which, her mother had replied succinctly, "Trollop!"

Later, visibly upset, her father had come to see her. He had told her he would not force her to marry Winchester, but for her mother's sake, she would be sent home for good. At the time, it had sounded too good to be true. But as the years passed and her mother's barbs—though less frequent these days—kept the shame alive, Chastity had begun to long for escape.

Standing in the formal garden now, gazing at the stone terrace, she shuddered. "Come on, Chastity," she told herself, "only six more months. You can last six more months."

She heard Buster's excited bark as he spied her. She turned to watch him run from the trees. Alex remained where he was, his white shirt in sharp contrast to the woods. His eyes never left hers. The dog ran back to Alex, then again to Chastity's side, as if urging them to close the gap that lay between them.

Chastity turned and headed for the house.

Alex followed more slowly, his route taking him across the green lawn, past the gazebo. He wasn't paying any attention to where he was going.

"Watch it, old man, you'll move my croquet ball."

"What?" Alex answered sharply.

Sir Charles grinned. "Methinks I shouldn't play cards with you any time soon. You know what they say— lucky at cards, unlucky at love."

"What the deuce are you going on about, Charlie? And why are you playing croquet in December?"

"Why not? It's warm enough. Besides, there are other diversions to be had when one is matched against certain people." He nodded toward the gazebo where Lady Costain was standing at the doorway straightening her gown. When she saw Alex, she disappeared inside. "And you needn't rip up at me just because *your* partner likes a more experienced man. What was it? Move too fast or too slow? Let me in on the secret; I'll . . . *ow!*"

Alex glared down at his old friend and said, "I warned you not to go on about such rubbish, Charlie. Next time I'll do more than draw your cork!"

Chapter Three

Chastity was not looking forward to this ball; it would be like all the rest. She would sit with the chaperones whenever her mother had no errands for her to attend to, and she would be bored.

She had eaten her dinner in her room rather than join the rest of the guests. She had fully expected her mother to protest, but it hadn't happened. Instead, her mother had told her sisters that it would be an excellent idea for them, too. That way they could make a dramatic entrance.

So Chastity was allowed a further period of peace before facing Alex again. She had spent the remainder of the afternoon berating herself for blowing a simple kiss out of proportion, but in her experience, she was unable to dismiss it as unimportant. She told herself she should be angry with him, but again, her experience had taught her that only she was to blame that the kiss had occurred. She had been too intimate in her conversation; she had failed to keep him at arm's length; she had been forward. Once again, she told herself sternly, she had failed to live up to her name.

Still, the time came to dress for the ball, and she could think of no excuse (that her mother would accept), to remain in her room. So, she put on her bravest face and determined to survive the Christmas ball.

The comtesse was the first to arrive, and she was pounced upon immediately by the gentlemen, Chastity noted with amusement. The Frenchwoman's heavy perfume permeated the air, and Chastity watched in awe as she managed to wrap every man present around her long, elegant fingers. Even Alex, or rather, Mr. Fitzsimmons, was not immune to her obvious flirting. One by one, the men bowed and smiled that vacuous smile, as the comtesse singled out each one for special attention.

She was not amazingly beautiful, decided Chastity, studying the older woman objectively. Rather, it was her attitude. It was as if she were bestowing a special gift on each man simply by speaking to him. And they lapped it up like kittens did cream.

The other guests began to arrive. There were twenty-five "neighbors," some traveling from as far away as Hastings. A small orchestra tuned their instruments in the musicians' gallery above the elegant ballroom.

Chastity wore a gown of crimson and white. It was new, her mother having insisted that all three girls have the very latest style for the ball. Tranquility and Sincerity were dressed in the palest blue and pink, the fabrics glistening like moonlight.

Chastity's gown of deep crimson silk was a striking contrast. The high waistline and scooped neckline her mother had declared *de rigueur* this season suited Chastity's height. She looked elegant and sophisticated.

By contrast, the style made her sisters look like little girls or dolls. Pocket Venuses, that would be the term everyone applied to them, their doting mother had exclaimed. Normally, this type of pronouncement was followed by a brisk "tsk" as Chastity was inspected. But tonight had been different. Her mother had been taken aback by her eldest's appearance; she had even said, "You're looking quite well tonight, Chastity."

Perhaps it was this tidbit of approval that gave Chastity boldness. She smiled more, greeting their neighbors with genuine pleasure. And when the second set of dancers formed, and Mr. Peaches requested her hand, she accepted gladly.

Alex appeared on the threshold of the ballroom, his good looks causing a rash of whispering among hopeful mothers and their daughters.

He approached Lady Costain and said, "Good evening, Lady Costain. You're not dancing?"

"No, I've just rejoined the ball."

"Then perhaps you'll do me the honor of allowing me to sit with you."

"Certainly, Mr. Fitzsimmons," gushed the lady, moving her skirts to one side. "Such a pretty spectacle, isn't it?"

"The dancers? Rather like a kaleidoscope."

"Miss Tranquility is certainly in looks tonight."

Taking the hint, Alex said gallantly, "I hadn't noticed anyone else's beauty."

The practiced Lady Costain pretended to blush behind her fan, saying, "Oh, you are outrageous, I vow."

Alex was supposed to make a witty rejoinder, but the steps of the dance had brought Chastity into his view, and he stared at her unabashedly. She was smiling at Peaches, her cheeks fused with a delicate blush, her hair piled atop her head and entwined with white rosebuds. The deep red of her gown lit up her green eyes as she glanced his way.

"Oh dear, I've dropped my fan," said Lady Costain, masking her indignation at his inattention. He bent down and returned it and his attention to her.

Lady Costain lowered her voice and leaned toward him provocatively. "Sad, isn't it?"

"What is that, my lady?"

"About the eldest Hartford gel."

"I see nothing sad about her."

"Oh, one can't see it. But still, it is indelibly written on her soul." With this, one gloved hand fluttered to her breast, the movement designed to draw his eyes to her charms.

But Alex was not tempted. "I'm surprised someone of your obvious intelligence and discernment would believe such old, idle gossip," he said slowly, forcing an admiring smile.

"Why, I . . . Of course I don't believe it. I never did!"

"Ah, good! They're forming a new set. I know it is bold of me to monopolize you for two dances, but please say you'll do me the honor."

She agreed instantly, forgetting all about spreading petty rumors as he showered her with compliments.

Chastity stood up with her father next; basking in his approval, her face became animated. Gentlemen watching made note of her beauty, suddenly wondering why they'd not noticed the eldest Hartford girl's attractions on earlier visits.

"I asked Cook about her daughter today, Papa, and about James," said Chastity.

"Hale tells me he's doing a fine job in the stables."

"Good. I hope that will keep him . . . you know," said Chastity. Her father nodded. "Anyway, I told Cook to make some goodies, and I'd take them a basket. She thought that was a good idea. I was wondering what else you think I should include."

"Some fresh fruit and vegetables from the hothouses, and I'll find a suitable bottle of brandy for James. Something for the baby, too. It's due any time, is it not?"

"Around the New Year," she said. "Cookie is so excited, but Jane being her youngest child, she's a little bit afraid, too, I think."

"I'm sure everything will be fine; babies usually have a way of arriving without any problems. Cook's a good woman, but she worries too much. I only hope her son-in-law keeps out of trouble."

"He will, Papa. He loves the horses, and he's very good with them, even with Baby, and you know he's one horse who has well-defined tastes."

"You and that stallion!" teased her father.

The music ended, and Chastity left her father for her next partner. Alex surrendered Lady Costain to Sir Charles, whose lip was visibly swollen.

"My dear man! What happened?" she asked anxiously.

"A horse kicked me. A mule, to be precise," he said, looking at Alex.

"Oh dear! How dreadful!" exclaimed her ladyship. "When did it happen? After our game?"

"Yes, and it has made me feel quite faint," he said weakly, allowing Lady Costain to lead him to a nearby sofa.

"Good evening, Mr. Fitzsimmons," said a husky voice with a heavy French accent.

Alex turned and smiled. "Good evening, comtesse. Have I told you yet how lovely you look tonight?"

She trilled with laughter and sidled closer. "And even if I had not spent hours at my toilette so that I might look lovely, you would be obliged to say so, monsieur." Alex raised a brow. "Oh, but I am being naughty, aren't I? I am not playing the game by the rules. I should say, 'Oh, la, sir, you'll turn my head.'"

The comtesse paused, allowing Alex a chance to respond. "Let us say you are being French, rather than naughty, my dear comtesse. We English set great store by these silly little games."

"Do I not know it, sir?" She surveyed the dance floor. "Look there at our host, Lord Hartford. He is a dear man, but one gets the feeling he has learned his part by rote. It is the same with Lord Ravenwood and Mr. Oxworth. Now, your friend Sir Charles, he is different; he is, I would say, irreverent."

"And I?" asked Alex, intrigued.

"Why you, monsieur, are a man of singular perception, a man to be reckoned with, a man to respect."

"You are too kind," he said quietly, a slight frown on his face. Her words were complimentary, but he felt uneasy about them, about her. "The musicians are beginning another tune. Would you do me the honor?"

"Alas, I have given this dance to our host. Another time?"

"Of course," said Alex as Lord Hartford claimed the comtesse. He shrugged off the feeling of . . . How could he define it? Uneasiness was not it. No, there was something oddly repellent about her.

He watched her with Lord Hartford. If he was playing a role, then so was she—her smiles, the tilt of her head, all looked studied, planned.

Alex frowned fiercely; she was the one playing a role. And her purpose? Could it extend to espionage? What better way to become accepted by a neighborhood, including the local magistrate, than to play the role of a rich, foreign, *femme fatale*.

Perhaps she was his man, so to speak, he told himself. The next time he rode out at night, he would position himself closer to her estate.

Alex was distracted by Chastity, the steps of the dance taking her past him. She really was looking magnificent tonight, he thought. She was so regal, so elegant. Just watching her made his pulse race.

Alex shook his head, wishing he could clear his mind as easily. What was he thinking of? he asked himself. The last thing he needed was to become embroiled with Chastity Hartford. Not only would it interfere with his job, but it might even prove dangerous! He needed to stay sharp!

Chastity passed again, and Alex felt his resolve slipping. Besides, as soon as he finished his assignment here, he was going back to the Peninsula. At least, he planned to; not immediately, perhaps, he amended, watching her dip a curtsey to her partner as the dance ended.

Chastity left the dance floor and sought a nearby chair; it was the first dance she had sat out all evening. She smiled at the two young ladies next to her and had the dubious honor of being snubbed by these less fortunate young ladies. They tossed their heads and moved away. They were neighbors, but their friendship did not allow for Chastity's being more sought after than they.

It was almost time for the supper dance, one of the few dances empty on her card. This didn't trouble her; no doubt her mother would have all sorts of duties for her to carry out. A shadow fell across the card, and a strong, tanned hand reached for it.

"You are very popular tonight, Chastity. I've not been able to get near you."

"I hadn't noticed," she said tartly.

Alex sat down beside her and started to write his name on the card. "Will you share supper with me?" At her alarmed expression, he said hastily, "If it's about this afternoon—I beg of you, Chastity, forgive me. It was the memories, you see. When you asked about Spain . . . I just wanted to block everything out. I didn't mean to frighten you. Say you'll forgive me, even though I don't deserve it," he added persuasively.

Chastity relented and smiled at him. She found it impossible to remain angry with him. It was the excitement, the success of the ball, she told herself. Alex again picked up the card, but Chastity stopped him.

"I'd like to, but I . . ." Chastity's eyes darted around

the room until she found her mother's hard gaze resting on her.

Alex's eyes followed hers. "Would it pose a problem for you?"

"No, not me, only ... My ... That is, Tranquility ..."

"I see," said Alex. He saw more than she knew. He wrote in his name for the dance following supper and returned her card. Then he stood up, took her hand, and lifted it to his lips, the noble gesture bringing Chastity both pleasure and pain.

Alex disappeared quickly, and Chastity sank back in her chair. The evening had suddenly gone flat; she wanted nothing more than to seek the solace of her room. She rose, but her progress was impeded by Ruben Oxworth.

"Miss Chastity, might an old man beg the honor of sharing supper with you?"

"Why, I don't know. I ..." How could she accept when she had already turned Alex down.

"Mr. Fitzsimmons is partnering your sister Tranquility, and I thought the four of us might share a table."

Chastity's green eyes flew open at this, and she looked past her father's friend to see Alex writing in Tranquility's card.

"That sounds wonderful, Mr. Oxworth," she said quickly, and waited while he wrote down his name. "If you'll excuse me for a moment ..."

Then she fled to her room, needing time to check her excitement, to reflect on the reason behind it.

But Chastity's smiling image in the glass wouldn't allow serious reflection. She was at a Christmas ball, she was dancing almost every dance, her scavenger hunt partner—(he was so perceptive!)—had arranged to dine with her without angering her mother, and she would not question. She would simply enjoy.

* * *

The supper dance was a Boulanger, and Chastity had to concentrate on the steps. Each time she met up with Ruben, he took the opportunity to extoll her sister Tranquility's charms. Other partners would have been furious, but Chastity was amused.

"She is so petite, so pretty. I'm sure she will be the toast of London next spring," he said.

"And Sincerity, too, I suppose, since they are identical," said Chastity with a laugh.

He frowned, considering this as the steps of the dance separated them again.

When they came back together, he continued, "As to that, I'm not certain. Surely a young lady's personality counts for something. And while Sincerity is charming, too, she lacks a certain vitality."

The dull Sincerity passed by them just then, a trill of laughter floating after her.

"Could it be, Mr. Oxworth, that you are simply more taken by my sister Tranquility?"

His dark skin turned darker, and he ducked his head like a schoolboy. Chastity had mercy on him and changed the subject as the music came to an end.

The sumptuous repast her mother had planned was pounced on by the guests with glee. Champagne flowed freely—not champagne punch as was served by some of the hostesses in the neighborhood, but real French champagne.

As Alex lifted his glass and sipped the sparkling liquid, he pictured the smugglers' boats landing with the bootlegged cargo destined for the local magistrate's cellars. He looked across the room and caught the eye of Lord Hartford, who raised his glass to Alex in a silent toast. Alex nodded and sipped the champagne. Hartford was hard to figure. The man was an amiable host, putting forth suggestions for his guests' entertainment, but never forcing it on them.

Alex's gaze traveled farther, and he shook his head as his eyes came to rest on Lady Hartford. She was still a handsome woman, but he found her behavior intolerable. To his way of thinking, Hartford deserved a medal for staying with his wife.

Of course, Lord Hartford did have his mistress in London. Intelligence had told him so, and Alex had met her, too, on the pretense of mistaking her house for that of a friend's. She was a sympathetic, gray-haired woman in her late forties, he judged—hardly the typical light o' love. He wondered if Chastity knew of the relationship.

Alex returned his attention to his table where Oxworth was entertaining Tranquility by folding a piece of note paper into the form of a bird. But Chastity was watching him, her expression troubled. Alex smiled, and she responded.

"This is quite the London ball," he said, with a sweep of his hand. "Your mother is an excellent hostess."

"Thank you," said Chastity. "She organizes things very well."

"Things and people," he said sagely.

"Perhaps," she conceded. Chastity looked at her sister and Oxworth, who was oblivious to everyone and everything around them. "My mother does like to have control of situations. For instance, she probably disapproves of our foursome here, but she can do nothing about it since I am officially Mr. Oxworth's partner."

Alex grinned. "I had thought of that."

"I know, and I appreciate your diplomacy." Afraid she had gone too far, been speaking in too forward a manner, she added, "Not that I wouldn't have had a partner."

"Of course not."

"I usually just help out, making sure all the dishes are

kept full, and all the guests are happy. My mother depends on my help."

"I'm sure she does. But isn't it pleasant simply to be one of the guests?" he asked, leaning forward in an intimate manner.

"How is everyone doing?" said Lady Hartford, swooping down on them suddenly.

"Fine, Mama. Look what Mr. Oxworth made for me!" said Tranquility, holding up two paper birds.

"How sweet of him," said her mother. "After supper, Chastity, I need you to . . ."

"Dance with me, my lady," interrupted Alex with what was meant to be a disarming grin, but was received with a chilly frown by his hostess. "I've got the next dance."

"Very well," said her ladyship reluctantly. "But after that, come and see me, Chastity."

"Yes, Mother."

Lady Hartford left them and fell on the next table. Chastity breathed a sigh of relief.

Calling her back to him, Alex said, "Chastity, I look forward to your opinion on my dancing after supper. I think I'm doing better; my leg seems to be getting stronger every day."

"Oh, la, Mr. Fitzsimmons, you mustn't speak to a lady about your leg!" simpered Tranquility, tapping him on the arm with the ease of a practiced flirt. "Why, only look how you've made Chastity's cheeks flame. I daresay she's blushing all the way down to her toes—if I were permitted to mention toes in front of gentlemen," she added audaciously.

"Tranquility!" chided Ruben Oxworth with an indulgent laugh.

She made moue and said, "You know I'm only teasing, Ruben. Chastity knows that."

Chastity looked up at this, stared her sister in the eye

and said, "Yes, I do know, Tranquility. I'm accustomed to it by now. But I see everyone is returning to the ballroom. Perhaps we should, too."

They rose and Chastity turned to Ruben, but Alex stepped between them.

"Permit me, Chastity. After all, we do have the next dance," he said, and took her hand, placing it on his arm. When they had left the other two behind, he leaned closer and said, "I only wanted to tell you I thought I might try riding tomorrow morning and wondered if you would care to accompany me." So much for your self-control, old man, Alex told himself.

"I'm not sure," she said frankly. At his raised brow, she explained, "I have an errand to do, and Mother has an outing planned for all of us, to the lighthouse and castle at Dover."

"Really? Right after the ball?" said Alex, astounded.

"My mother expects her house party to be entertaining—no matter how fatiguing it may be," quipped Chastity.

"Perhaps we could go around nine, if you think you'll be up. I thought we might see about getting that mail coach whip, but I may have to settle for a gallop along the beach. It's been years since I've done that."

"It does sound tempting, but you mustn't overdo, Mr. Fitzsimmons."

"What happened to Alex?" he teased.

"Not here," she said, unable to meet his eyes.

"Very well, but you'll go?" She nodded her assent and he added, "Then it's all settled. We'll meet in the hall at nine o'clock."

A shadow crossed Chastity's eyes. "Let's meet at the stables," she said quietly, searching the gathering for her mother. "And I do have to deliver a basket to one of our tenants, if you don't mind accompanying me."

Alex gave a slight bow and led her into the quadrille that was forming.

Alex slipped out of the crowded ballroom as soon as he had given Chastity to her next partner. He made his way past the stables and entered the gray stallion's paddock. Silently, he led the horse beyond the yard. Here, behind the fence, he uncovered a hidden bridle and slipped it over the big horse's head. He swung up, barebacked, and was soon away.

Alex rode as fast as he could through the woods, having a little trouble finding the spot where the stone fence had fallen between the two estates so that he could pass through. He saw the lights of the Frenchwoman's house and dismounted, tethering the stallion in a patch of sweet clover.

Stealthily, Alex made his way toward the old stone manor house. He found the door that led to his godfather's old study and let himself in silently. He paused inside, allowing his eyes time to adjust. It was darker inside than it had been outside with the moon to guide him. He felt along the wall for the entrance to the library.

Inside this room, he was surprised to find a feeble fire in the grate. He froze, his eyes searching for the room's occupant. Satisfied that he was alone, he went toward the desk, which was strewn with papers. He glanced through these quickly, dismissing them. He tried the drawers and found they were all open, their contents equally uninteresting. He heard a clock somewhere strike three.

Alex moved toward the door that led to the back hall. He opened it and listened. All was quiet. He crept along the hall to the front of the house, hesitating only a second before mounting the wide staircase that led to the bedrooms.

The first one he entered was obviously unoccupied. Next, he tried the master bedroom. Here, the bed was turned down, and a hearty fire burned in the grate. Alex first tried the small secretary in the corner, but it was empty. Discouraged, he opened the wardrobe. Pushing aside the clothes, he frowned. Nothing.

He shut the door and went into the dressing room. There was a trunk on the floor, its fasteners ornate and shining. He opened it, rifling through the contents rapidly before pausing, his forehead wrinkled by a thoughtful frown. He let the clothing fall from his fingers; quickly, he searched the other armoire in the room. Six or eight gowns hung from hooks, but Alex ignored them.

"I tell you, Jean-Jacques, someone was in the study! Do I not always leave the same letter on top?" said a voice in French from the bedroom. It was the comtesse.

"Perhaps the wind . . ." offered the servant.

Alex paused only a moment before moving toward the fireplace.

"I want you to rouse Remi and search the grounds."

"You are crazy; I would know if anyone entered. Besides, who would do so? Hartford? That Lieutenant Humphries? They are both too stupid!"

"Never mind who. Just see to it!" ordered the comtesse. The door to the dressing room opened, and she slipped inside.

From behind the secret panel beside the fireplace, Alex watched the comtesse discard her gown, replacing it with a sensible nightgown. As the unveiling continued, he grinned despite himself, wondering what Hartford and Charlie would say if they were there. They would feel the proper fools, that was for certain.

Alex remained where he was until the comtesse had

left the room. Then, silently, he made his way down the hidden stairs behind the walls that led to the outside. He thanked his stars for his explorations when he was only a youth that had led to this discovery. It had very likely saved his life.

Outside, he heard the grumbling servants as they began their search of the grounds. When they had turned the corner and were out of sight, he sprinted across the overgrown lawn and into the underbrush. He led Baby halfway back to the fallen wall before mounting and riding back to the Hartford's estate.

Chastity tossed and turned, berating herself for her stupidity. She should never have agreed to go riding with Alex Fitzsimmons, and not because her mother might find out.

She was certain he knew about her past. That was the only possible explanation for his invitation.

Perhaps not, another voice said, a hopeful voice she rarely listened to. Perhaps Alex was different; perhaps he only wanted her friendship.

No, the other voice argued, men didn't choose unmarried females as friends; they chose them as mistresses.

Chastity wondered what she would do if Alex offered her his protection. She would not accept, of course, but she would be sorry to lose his friendship. She was beginning to care for him, and it was not that wild infatuation she had felt at fourteen. It was more; it was as if she had met a kindred spirit, and she would miss him.

Impatiently, Chastity wiped away a tear. There would be none of that! she told herself as she stared out the window at the half moon. It was beautiful the way it bathed the yard in soft moonlight. From her window, she could look out at the formal gardens beyond the terrace. To the left, she could see the paddocks and the stable yard.

She straightened up, her desultory examination changing on the instant. That was Baby, she realized in alarm. But he was not in his paddock. Someone was leading him into the stable yard.

With lightning speed, Chastity grabbed her wrapper and flew out of her room, down the back stairs, and into the kitchen gardens. She ducked behind the spruce tree as she heard the gate's hinges squeak.

Hardly daring to breathe, she waited. The footsteps drew nearer, passed, and entered the house. Chastity expelled the breath she had been holding.

Alex!

Chapter Four

"How does it feel?" asked Chastity the next morning after Alex was seated astride his horse. Through a great effort, she managed to keep the sarcasm from her voice.

Alex waved his crop in the air and said, "It's wonderful to be up on a horse again! Let's go!"

He had never seen her in better looks. Except, perhaps, he corrected himself, at the ball. Or when he had first spied her, stuck in the mud, dirty and disheveled. He looked at her again. No, that rust velvet habit just did something for her.

"We'll take it easy at first," she said.

Alex nodded. She had no idea he had been taking her horse out at night, riding him to the cliff overlooking the smugglers' cove. Then again, she had no idea his injury had long since healed. His use of the cane had only been part of his story, an extension of his excuse for having left the army.

They left the stable yard at a walk, and maintained it all the way down the drive, to the road. Strapped to the back of Chastity's saddle was the basket destined for Cook's daughter.

"Where are we going?" asked Alex.

"To take this basket to Jane and James Williams. James is one of our grooms; you've probably met him."

"Yes, he's been looking after a sore on one of my grays. He's very good with the horses."

"That's him. His wife is our cook's daughter. She's increasing; the baby is due in less than a month," said Chastity, knowing her mother would not approve of such an intimate topic for their conversation. But Chastity cared little for what she considered foolish taboos, and with Alex, she felt no fear of speaking her mind.

They rode into the yard of a neat thatched cottage and were greeted by a disinterested hound. His lazy "woof" brought a very pregnant girl to the door, as Alex helped Chastity down.

"Miss Hartford, how nice to see you. Come in, do."

"How are you, Jane?"

"I'm well, thank you, miss," she said, smiling.

"Let me present Alex Fitzsimmons. He was gracious enough to act as my escort."

Alex nodded cordially as he untied the basket from the back of Chastity's saddle.

Jane managed an awkward curtsey and ushered them inside. The room was tiny but spotless, containing a table and three chairs, an easy chair, and a fireplace. Chastity was shown to the easy chair, and Alex pulled two chairs up from the table. He handed Jane the basket.

"You shouldn't have, Miss Hartford," said the girl with a blush as she looked through the basket eagerly.

"It's from your mother, too. She and I put it together. There's a little gown for the baby, and some of your mother's famous cakes." As Jane pulled out the bottle of brandy, Chastity added, "And my father wanted James to have that. That husband of yours has made himself practically indispensable around the stables. He's a good worker."

"I know that; he's always working around here, fixing this or improving that. I think he's going to be alright."

They stayed long enough to drink a cup of tea and share a cake from the basket. Wishing Jane a happy Christmas and receiving a promise that she'd send word as soon as the baby arrived, they took their leave.

As they rode off at a sluggish walk, Alex said dryly, "I think we can pick it up a bit."

"I'm not convinced," said Chastity, tilting her head to one side, studying him.

"Let's just see who can reach the beach first."

Chastity drew back on the reins, and her stallion threw his head up in protest. "I don't think you should, Alex. Alex!"

He kicked up his horse, a gelding with half the speed of Chastity's stallion. Seconds later, he could hear rapid hoofbeats as Baby began to close the gap.

By the time they reached the beach, Chastity was four lengths ahead. She pulled up slowly and turned her stallion to watch Alex's approach. Her cheeks were flushed and her riding hat slightly askew; she looked adorable. But Alex didn't say that, of course.

"Why the devil do you call that huge beast such an absurd name as Baby?"

Chastity smiled and patted the stallion's neck. "But that's what he is—to me, at least. If anyone else tries to ride him . . ." She made a motion to signify the fall of a rider.

"I'll lay you a monkey I can do it," said Alex.

"I don't know what a monkey is, but I bet you can't," she said, slipping effortlessly to the ground. Of course you can, she wanted to say. You've taken him out before, without my permission, without my knowledge. But I know now.

Alex dismounted and went to stand at the stallion's head. He looked at the sidesaddle doubtfully.

"Not in that thing."

"Then take it off," said Chastity, moving back a little,

wishing heartily that her horse would live up to his reputation this one time and pitch Alex into the English
Channel.

Alex removed the side-saddle and prepared to swing
up onto the big stallion's back. Baby sidled away.

"Do you want me to hold him for you?" called Chastity.

"No, I can manage," said Alex. The horse again
moved away, and Alex said sourly, "You could at least
hold his bridle."

With a gurgle of laughter, Chastity moved to the
horse's head, her presence calming him. Alex vaulted
onto the horse's back. Baby swung his huge head
around and sniffed. Bite him, thought Chastity.

"Come on, boy, let's go for a little ride."

Chastity stood back and watched in amazement as
Baby was put through his paces, down the beach and
back.

"Nothing to it," said Alex, slipping to the ground.

"I wouldn't have believed it if I hadn't seen it with
my own eyes," said Chastity, holding the stallion while
Alex replaced the sidesaddle. "You really do have a way
with animals. It's hard to believe this is your first time to
ride him," she added, waiting to see if he would catch
her meaning. He didn't.

"That's what they say. Now, about that monkey . . ."

"I told you it was only a bet . . . no money."

"But one has to win something when one wins a bet,"
said Alex softly, moving closer to Chastity.

Despite herself, Chastity felt a thrill of excitement, but
she wasn't afraid. She was in control of herself and the
situation this time, and she had no intention of kissing
or being kissed by Alex Fitzsimmons again.

"Very well. The next time we race, you may ride
Baby," she said after a moment of consideration.

Alex laughed. "Fair enough! Now we had better get

back before anyone discovers our absence." He cupped his hands for her to mount.

Chastity found herself seated backward beside Lady Ravenwood and opposite her mother and Emma Bishop. Alex took Tranquility up in his curricle while Sincerity and Lord Ravenwood rode in another. Lady Costain and Sir Charles were also paired off. The remaining gentlemen rode on horseback. A dogcart piled with delicacies had been sent ahead so they could picnic beneath the ruins.

"Read to us, Chastity," commanded her mother, handing Chastity a guidebook.

"The lighthouse at Dover is of Roman times, built in the first century A.D. There are also the remains of an ancient fort, believed to be of Roman origin, too.

"Nearby is Dover Castle, a structure built in 1100 by the Normans. It was . . ."

"That's enough, gel. We don't want a deuced history lesson," barked old Lady Ravenwood.

Chastity closed the guidebook with a decided snap, and her mother threw her a warning look. Pasting a false smile on her face, Chastity mentally readied herself for a tiring day.

It was not improved when the comtesse rode up on a magnificent bay just before they turned into the road.

"Oh, Lady Hartford, I was just riding over to thank you for last night. What a delightful soirée it was!"

Lady Hartford gritted her teeth and smiled. "You are too kind," she finally managed to say.

Chastity didn't smile, but her eyes twinkled as the exchange continued. The comtesse was dressed in a severely cut riding habit of scarlet superfine. Her hat was a confection of lace and netting with a red plume that curled under her chin.

"But you are going out, I see."

"Yes, I had planned a little picnic for my house guests at the old lighthouse."

"How delightful! I have always adored picnics!"

It was inevitable. Her mother was forced to issue the invitation, her voice tight and her smile patently false.

"You are too kind! Thank you! *Merci!*" The comtesse trotted off and joined the men who were on horseback.

Just as she had planned, thought Chastity, who guessed correctly that the comtesse had heard about the proposed picnic and had made sure she would intercept them.

"Bonjour, messieurs," said the comtesse, bestowing a wicked smile on each gentleman.

"Impressive beast, comtesse," commented Ruben Oxworth.

"He is a dear, you know," she gushed.

"Quite a handful, I should think," said the older man doubtfully as the gelding sidled closer to Alex's curricle.

Ignoring Tranquility's presence in the vehicle, the comtesse leaned over and said huskily to Alex, "And do you like my pet, Monsieur Fitzsimmons?"

"Indeed, madam, but he seems to be favoring his right leg," said Alex observantly. "Perhaps you should have it looked at."

"It is his little way," she responded before smiling and riding ahead.

The house party paid only perfunctory attention to the Roman ruins and lighthouse. Lady Ravenwood quickly dismissed them as a frightful bore, and she dragged Chastity away. The main attraction of the outing was the picnic. Near the lighthouse, overlooking the sea, was a table laden with every delicacy of civilization. This was anything but a country picnic. Footmen in their blue livery stood at attention, ready to serve the hungry guests. There were blankets spread out on the ground here and there, or the guests could choose to sit at one of the tables with white linen cloths that had also been provided.

Not wishing to serve champagne again, Lady Hartford had ordered the best wines to accompany the stuffed crab, quails' eggs, raspberry trifle, and other dishes selected to tempt her guests. Chastity found her own appetite had fled, and she only picked at her food.

She watched as Alex made a perfect fool of himself, first serving the comtesse's plate and then feeding her slivers of thin turkey and strawberries dipped in chocolate. She wished she could hear their conversation, which would be laced, no doubt, with unsavory endearments.

In reality, Alex was doing very little talking, posing what he hoped was a leading question here or there about France and the comtesse's family. He received surprisingly little information. It was not that the comtesse refused to answer, but rather that she evaded, using her handkerchief to advantage, wiping away imaginary tears at any mention of either family or country. For Alex, it served to confirm his suspicions.

When they had finished their plates, the comtesse was claimed by Lord Costain, whose wife was deep in conversation with Sir Charles.

Chastity found herself captured by Lady Ravenwood, whose terse comments and outrageous observations managed to both irritate and intrigue her. How, Chastity wondered, could the old woman get away with saying (in a carrying voice), that since Ruben Oxworth was so wealthy he should think about buying a chin, and that the Frenchwoman's charms certainly didn't include a bosom. It almost made up for the fact that Alex was spending his time glued to the comtesse.

The other men, too, were drawn by that husky laugh, their eyes often drifting toward the figure in red. The ladies' gazes would follow, too, but their expressions were decidedly hostile.

It was as the final course was being cleared that Chastity found herself the object of Lady Ravenwood's piercing gaze.

"Miss, eh? Why Miss Hartford?"

"Pardon, my lady?" said Chastity warily.

"Why Miss? Why aren't you married yet? You're certainly old enough, and you're not ugly."

Chastity blinked, uncertain how to respond. She focused on the last phrase and said, "It is kind of you to say so, my lady, but . . ."

"No, it isn't. I'm never kind. That's the wonderful thing about being old, rich, and a widow. I don't have to please anyone," she said, shaking her finger at Chastity. Then she turned that gnarled finger on herself and jabbed her bony chest. "Except me!"

"No, my lady," answered Chastity dutifully.

"But first, you've got to get married, my girl. Now, why don't you choose one of them?" She waved at the assembled party.

"Perhaps they've not asked me, my lady," said Chastity quietly, a blush spreading across her features.

"Hmph! You've got to bring 'em up to scratch, girl! That's up to you! Now, which one d'you fancy? Not my grandson; he's too silly for you! How about Oxworth? Oh, I know he's chinless, but you could overlook that."

Chastity shook her head and dared not look up.

"What about Sir Charles? No? Then I guess it's got to be Fitzsimmons. Too bad about that limp, but maybe he'll outgrow it. So, Fitzsimmons it is! I'll just put a flea in his ear."

She started to rise, and Chastity tugged at her skirt, unable to speak.

"What's the matter with you, girl?"

"Please, my lady, don't," she whispered.

"Now, with you so shy, how else is Fitzsimmons supposed to know which way the wind sits?"

"Please . . ."

"Did you call my name, Lady Ravenwood? May I be of assistance?"

"Yes, I want to talk to you, young man."

"Alex, I really want to get a closer look at that lighthouse," said Chastity, rising suddenly and taking his arm, dragging him away from Lady Ravenwood.

"That's the way, girl!" called her ladyship with a cackle.

When they reached the base of the lighthouse, Chastity stopped and looked back. Lady Ravenwood waved, and Chastity dropped Alex's arm and slipped inside.

Alex followed and said, "Would you mind telling me what that was all about?"

Chastity glared at him. "That was about a rude old woman who hasn't got enough sense to stay out of other people's business!"

"Hey! I didn't have anything to do with it!" he protested, holding up his hands.

Chastity grimaced, knowing she should acknowledge this, but she was not ready to be reasonable. Besides, she told herself stubbornly, Alex had taken her horse without permission or explanation.

"She certainly upset you. What did she say?"

"Never mind. It was nonsense." She motioned toward the stairs, which looked none too safe. "Have you ever climbed to the top? It's clear enough to see for miles today."

"No, but I'd like to. Care to accompany me?" he asked, placing one foot on the first step and holding out his hand in invitation.

"I shouldn't," said Chastity, thinking how angry her mother would be.

"Come on. At least we'll be away from her for a little while," said Alex.

Chastity wasn't sure if he was referring to her mother or Lady Ravenwood, but either way, the temptation was too great, and she took his hand.

They reached the top, and Alex walked to the edge and leaned over, looking down.

"Be careful!" she hissed, realizing for the first time that she really didn't like being so high up. As a child, with her father, it had seemed like a great lark; now, she was less sure.

"Don't worry; the railing is sturdy," said Alex, leaning against this structure, causing Chastity to gasp. "It looks like someone has been up here to reinforce it. Come here. I won't let you fall."

Chastity edged toward him, grasping his hand like a lifeline. She peeked over the edge, took a step back, and shook her head.

"Do you want to go down?" he asked.

Again Chastity shook her head. She wouldn't let it be said that she was a coward. She stepped closer, and Alex put a steadying arm around her waist. She looked over the edge at the rest of the party.

Tranquility, looking up, spied them and cried out, waving frantically. They watched as she and Sincerity pointed and then dragged Lord Ravenwood and Oxworth inside the structure, disappearing from view. Alex and Chastity soon heard their excited chatter as they mounted the staircase.

"Your sisters will soon be here. Do you want to go down?"

"No, why would you assume that?"

"I just thought you didn't get along very well with them. They like to tease you."

"I can stand their teasing, I assure you, Mr. Fitzsimmons."

"Mr. Fitzsimmons, is it? My, I have done something to nettle you. But I can't imagine what it might be."

"It's nothing, Alex. Really."

"Really? Then you wouldn't mind if I did this," he said, his voice suddenly soft and seductive. His arm around her waist tightened, and he pulled her closer.

Steeling herself, Chastity threw back her head and looked him in the eye. She was not yet ready to forgive him his mysterious late night ride, she told herself. And she refused to admit that his performance with the comtesse at lunch might be influencing her feelings.

"If you feel you must," she said dispassionately.

With this, or was it because the voices were drawing close, Alex released her.

"You are a puzzle, Chastity," he said quietly as her sisters burst upon the scene.

Chastity was exhausted, and her head ached abominably. When she requested her mother's permission to remain in her room for the evening, it was granted without an argument, so she knew she looked as wretched as she felt.

By the time the dressing bell sounded, she was asleep, intending to nap for several hours before rising and watching the stables.

The ball the previous evening combined with the day's picnic had obviously tired everyone. The tea tray was ordered by ten o'clock, and the occupants of the drawing room were yawning and bidding each other good night by eleven.

Alex went to his room, changed to a black coat and riding boots, and waited. By midnight, he let himself out of his room and down the back stairs.

He had a shadow.

Chastity, also dressed in dark colors, followed silently.

* * *

How dare he! Chastity thought crossly as she watched Alex swing up on her horse. She waited until he had led the stallion away from the stable yard before she went to the tack room. She saddled her sister's mare, located in the stall farthest from the grooms' quarters.

The third quarter moon was waning, and Chastity had some difficulty discovering Alex's path. She ducked branches, riding as fast as she dared through the trees. She quickly realized where Alex was going, and she almost turned back.

Let him keep his assignation, she told herself. What did she care?

Chastity pulled the reins taut, and the mare stopped obediently. Alex was just ahead; he had dismounted and was tying the stallion to a tree. Chastity did the same, cautiously edging closer on foot.

Alex was still, staring at the comtesse's house; suddenly he sprinted across the gardens and lawn, keeping low to the ground.

Chastity moved forward, frowning. When she reached her horse, she patted him in a distracted manner. What was the man doing? Surely there was no reason for such secrecy. It was not as if the comtesse had a husband to worry about.

He was just playing games, she decided crossly. Then she saw Alex skulking amongst the shrubbery, finally disappearing into the house. She watched as a candle was lit. Then it went out.

Chastity wanted very much to take her horse and go home, stranding Alex. But then, Alex would know he had been followed, and she felt instinctively that there was more to the story.

You're being foolish! she told herself. You simply don't want to believe he is lying in the arms of the comtesse! But of course he was! Had he not spent most of the afternoon with her? They had probably planned it all then!

Unwilling to examine the reasons for her low spirits, Chastity rode home on her sister's mare, softly humming a tune to occupy her thoughts, to keep them from turning to Alex and the comtesse.

Chastity had thought she would be awake all night, but her exhaustion was such that she fell fast asleep. Her dreams were troubled; she found herself both searching for Alex and fleeing from him.

Waking before nine with burning eyes, Chastity dressed and made her way outdoors, peeping around corners and ducking behind shrubbery in her efforts to avoid Alex. She went to the gazebo and slipped inside, sinking down on the nearest cushioned bench. Within minutes, she was asleep again.

Chastity woke with a start, her eyes flying open, having difficulty adjusting to the bright midday sun. She straightened up and gasped as her hand was seized.

"My dear Chastity, what a charming picture you present in repose."

"Sir Charles!" she said, wrenching her hand free. "You startled me!"

"I do beg your pardon, but when I spied you here, I was loath to leave you alone and unprotected."

He was a handsome man with his deep blue eyes and golden blond hair, but Chastity found him distasteful. She stood up and excused herself.

"But my dear girl, surely you will offer me some reward for my vigilance," he said, taking her hand again.

Chastity frowned. Her sisters would have turned away such an advance with titters and much batting of the eyes. Chastity, however, refused to resort to such tactics.

"I don't know what you mean," she said, very much afraid that she did know.

He was beside her now. He was quite as tall as Alex and looked down on her with a leer. One hand snaked out and rested heavily on her shoulder.

"Surely you can think of something, Chastity. A kiss will do for a start," he said seductively.

Chastity's chin went up defiantly, and she said fiercely, "Why don't you go and find Lady Costain. I'm sure she would welcome your advances. I find them revolting."

"And I find that hard to believe, Chastity." He made her name sound like a curse. "I mean, surely you cannot object to a little dalliance with a man of experience, Chastity. After all, I understand you were quite generous with Winchester!"

Chastity tore away from his grasp, stumbled through the open archway and fled toward the house, her horror propelling her faster and faster.

"Chastity!" someone called, but she continued blindly on. Alex's handsome brow was furrowed as he watched her flight.

"Skittish little thing," said his friend.

Alex turned to face Sir Charles, raw fury in his gaze. Charlie stepped back and put up his hands to ward off an attack.

"Charlie, leave."

"Alex, old man . . ." he began, trying to laugh.

"Today. Now."

"Love to oblige, old man, but . . ." Sir Charles sneered.

Alex's voice was quiet, deadly. "Don't do it as an obligation. Do it out of fear. I would tell you to leave out of decency, but you've obviously shaken off any shred of decency you ever possessed. And if I find, when I return to London, that you have sullied Chastity's name, I'll call you out and kill you. Hanging, be damned."

Sir Charles tried once again to laugh it off. "You act like you're her husband."

Alex raised his chin and narrowed his eyes. "As a matter of fact, I hope to be." He turned on his heel and followed Chastity.

He spied her hurrying up the steps of the terrace. Her mother stood at the top, her hands on her hips and a look of displeasure on her face. Hadn't Chastity been through enough already, thought Alex.

"Chastity! What am I going to do with you, running about like a hoyden! What were you thinking?"

"I'm sorry, Mother," Chastity said automatically. "I . . . I was playing with the dog." She heard giggling and looked at the table where Tranquility and Sincerity were both working on their embroidery.

"Well, sit down with your sisters and try to be a lady!"

"Yes, Mother," said Chastity, joining her sisters.

Their laughter subsided, and as they chattered about this and that, Chastity didn't move, her senses numb.

"Lord Ravenwood told me my eyes were as blue as a summer sky," Sincerity was saying.

"Very pretty. You'll never guess what Ruben told me," said Tranquility, inching forward and dropping her voice confidentially. "He told me he was going to speak to Father after next Season." She sat back triumphantly.

"Really! What will you say? He is awfully old!"

"Being a young widow wouldn't be so terrible," said Tranquility, adopting an air of worldly cynicism.

"Maybe not," agreed Sincerity callously. "But being married to one might not be so pleasant."

"True. I think I shall let him kiss me, just to see if I can tolerate it."

Chastity, who had been content to be ignored,

stretched out her hand and took Tranquility's in a tight grip.

"Don't!" she hissed. "Never let a man kiss you! It will ruin you!"

Her younger sisters exchanged speaking glances and smiled in a placatory manner.

"Surely, Chastity, one kiss . . ."

"No! Please believe me. I can't explain, but please, both of you, believe me!"

Tranquility was visibly affected by Chastity's vehemence, but she shook her head and said, "Sarah Goodson has kissed several gentlemen and no such fate befell her, Chastity. I know you mean well, but I think you exaggerate. One little kiss has never ruined a girl!"

"Yes, it will if anyone finds out."

"You sound like Mama," said Sincerity.

"A simple little kiss? I think you're over-reacting," said Tranquility.

"No, I'm not. That's what ruined me." With this, Chastity left them to stare at each other, dumbfounded.

"Is that why Mama says such awful things to her? Over a kiss?" said Sincerity, clearly shocked.

"I have heard Mama saying Chastity disgraced herself, but I assumed it was something much more shocking than a kiss," Tranquility said quietly, the depth of her sympathy bringing tears to her eyes.

"How awful!" whispered Sincerity.

Neither girl noticed the movement of the curtains at the French doors. Alex was quaking with anger—anger for Chastity, anger at her mother, and at an unforgiving society.

Alex found Lord Hartford hiding in the library, his feet propped up on a table, a copy of *Gentleman's Quarterly* open, but forgotten, on his chest.

"I'd like to speak to you, my lord," said Alex, closing the door.

Lord Hartford sat up and studied his serious young visitor with shrewd green eyes. He reminded Alex of his eldest daughter at that moment, a fact that hardened his resolve.

"What can I do for you, Alex? By the look of you, it must be important."

Alex had not planned to bring up his mission, but he knew suddenly that he could not broach his other topic until he had satisfied himself of Hartford's innocence.

"Lord Hartford, you may not be aware of the true purpose of my visit to Sussex."

"Really? And I thought it was a Christmas house party," said his lordship blandly.

Alex frowned. This was not the response he had anticipated. Lord Hartford held up a hand.

"I am not without my own connections, Fitzsimmons. I, too, travel to London from time to time. I am a member of the Lords, and being a magistrate in this area, I am closely concerned with the security of our coastline."

"Go on," said Alex, unwilling to reveal the details of his visit before learning what his host already knew.

"It was I who went to the Home Office with my concerns about the comtesse." At Alex's surprised expression, he nodded sagely. "They didn't bother to tell you that, did they?"

"No, they told me to suspect everyone."

"No doubt Lord Sheffield took my concerns to someone else, someone who neither knows me nor has any reason to trust me."

Alex grinned. "My contact told me to trust no one."

Hartford nodded his gray head and continued, "It's just as well. And I don't care whether you trust me or not. I know I'm not involved in any spy activity."

"But you do serve very good wine. French wine."

It was Lord Hartford's turn to smile. "I don't deny taking advantage of a bargain when it's offered, and I don't inquire into its source too closely. But I draw the line at espionage; so do most other people around here. As a matter of fact, I'm glad you came. Lieutenant Humphries is a good chap, but he knows very little about catching smugglers or spies. He sends that boat out almost every night, as if the men he's after are stupid enough to be caught by such clumsy methods."

"You sound as if you're well acquainted with them."

Hartford shook his head. "I was well acquainted with a few of them. Even honest families had a hand in the pie, so to speak. But they've been shoved out, or quit. There's more going on here than smuggling, and it started to change when she arrived," he said quietly, crooking his head in the direction of the comtesse's estate.

Alex was thoughtful. Finally, he took a deep breath, deciding to trust his host completely. "You're right about the comtesse. And I found receipts that implicate one or two local people, but most of them are French, I believe."

"Why don't you call in the militia?" said Lord Hartford, sitting forward eagerly.

"That would only drive them out of this area. They'd set it up somewhere else. I want the key men, even the ones in France. I'm fairly certain they travel back and forth regularly, but I never know when."

"How can you manage that?"

"I've got a plan. If I can get close enough to one of the locals."

Hartford was shaking his head. "Impossible. They'd never betray the brotherhood. For one thing, they don't want to hang. And having a knife stuck through your back one dark night is not a pleasant thought either. There's got to be another way."

"If you can think of something, I'd be happy to consider it."

Hartford sat in silence for several moments before a slow smile spread across his face. "What if I contacted one of the locals and told them I needed a big shipment? So big, they couldn't refuse, and by Christmas Eve. That would narrow down when you can expect them."

"It just might work. You'll have to hurry, though; it's only four more days," said Alex.

"As I said, it will narrow down the time in question. I'll ride into town this afternoon."

"I'll contact Lieutenant Humphries and tell him to withdraw his men and boats until I send for him," said Alex.

"Anything else I can do?"

"No, if you can set it up, I'll take care of the rest of it." Alex hesitated. He looked at the man before him, reflecting how simple the one topic had been and how difficult it was to broach the other. "There is one more thing. It has nothing to do with the other business." Still, Alex stalled.

"Chastity?" said Hartford, causing Alex to acknowledge his perception. "I may play least in sight around here, Alex, but I'm not blind, and I know my daughter."

"Do you? I wish I did. I haven't a clue as to how she feels about me. I only know I'd like a chance to . . . I have no right to ask now, not in the middle of all this. And even afterwards, I always planned to go back to Spain."

"Why don't you wait, Alex. Chastity's not going anywhere, and . . ."

There was a knock on the door, and a servant announced Sir Charles. Alex stood up and glared at his former friend.

"I'm afraid I've received an urgent message from my old aunt. She's taken it into her head that she wants me there for Christmas, and I don't dare displease her. I hope you'll forgive me and explain it all to your dear wife."

Ever the charmer, thought Alex with a snort of derision.

Hartford looked from one young man, his eyes like ice, to the other, whose eyes already showed lines of dissipation.

"Of course, Sir Charles," he said, playing the flawless host. "We shall certainly miss you, but I can see that it is unavoidable. I'll make your excuses to Lady Hartford. Good-bye," he said.

They shook hands and Sir Charles paused, looking at Alex. He held out his hand, his expression proud, but pleading. Alex looked down, then extended his hand and gave one firm shake.

"Good-bye, Alex. Good luck."

"Thanks, Charlie. I hope your aunt leaves you buckets of gold," he said, grinning.

"Oh, if only she would, but she'll probably outlive me!"

Alex spent the remainder of the afternoon searching for the militia lieutenant before finally running him to ground in Hastings. His credentials accepted, he had little difficulty persuading the peach-faced young man to agree to his scheme.

Returning to Hartford House, he barely had time to dress for dinner before joining the rest of the house party at the table. He reflected that although he was not allowed to sit beside Chastity, he did have the opportunity to study her across the table. She was very subdued, her eyes rarely leaving her plate, except once or twice to study the empty place left by Sir Charles. He wished he had been able to set her mind at rest, but that would have to wait till later.

After the interminable dinner, Alex was able, with Lord Hartford's help, to persuade the other gentlemen to join the ladies almost immediately. He entered the salon, his eyes travelling the length of the room to find the sofa empty. He quickly determined that she was absent and spent the next two hours alternately worrying about her and denouncing her for a coward. When he finally escaped, after much pointed yawning, he went straight to her room.

"Chastity, let me in."

Chastity swung her feet to the floor and stood up, unsure what to do next.

"It's me, Alex."

"I know," she said. "What do you want?"

"Open the door, will you?"

Chastity padded across the room, tying her wrapper around her tightly. She cracked the door and said, "You shouldn't be here. Go away."

"After we talk," he said, pushing inside and waiting for her to close the door. He was unprepared for the fear in her eyes and moved closer to offer her comfort. She flinched when he touched her arm.

"Alex, please go," she said, unable to raise her eyes. She knew it had been his voice she had heard as she staggered away from the gazebo. That he had been witness to her shame . . . It was intolerable!

Alex hid his agitation and dropped his hand. His voice hoarse with emotion, he said, "Charlie won't be back, and he won't be talking either."

Chastity shivered, but when he reached out to her, she backed away.

"I know he is your friend, but I couldn't like him."

"That's alright. I haven't liked him very much either this past week."

"He wrote me a note of apology."

"Did he? Then perhaps there are a few vestiges of decency left in him, though he'd probably knock me down for saying so." Alex ached to pull her to him as she shivered uncontrollably again. But he didn't dare. Nor did he dare tell her about his conversation with her father. Not now. That would have to wait.

Instead, he said brightly, "I thought we'd go and find that mail coach whip tomorrow morning, if you like. Time's running out, you know."

"I know. Very well, if you wish," Chastity managed to say.

"We'll meet at the stables at ten." He reached for the doorknob.

"Alex, wait."

"Yes?"

Chastity looked up, her green eyes large and puzzled. "Nothing. I was going to say, 'don't go', but then I remembered where we were." She gave him a tentative smile.

"You're right. I should go. It's late," he lied.

It must have showed because the smile faded, and the curtain over her eyes closed. "Of course. Good night."

"Good night, Chastity."

When he had gone, Chastity blew out the candles and took up her vigil at the window, staring at the gardens below, waiting for that shadowy figure to appear as he made his way to the comtesse.

Chastity was glad she had followed him. He had fooled her. His course that night had not taken him to the comtesse. He might be meeting her somewhere else, she told herself sensibly. Or he might not, that other voice said.

She was almost out of the woods when she saw him, Baby's pale gray coat glistening in the moonlight. They were moving at a rapid pace, along the tree line. Keeping her mare inside the trees, Chastity followed, the creek of saddle leather sounding deafening in her ears.

After some time, Alex pulled up and tied Baby to a tree. Then he proceeded on foot, making his way cautiously toward the edge of the cliffs. Chastity dismounted and walked toward the stallion, not daring to cross the open space for fear of detection.

Alex disappeared, and Chastity spent half an hour wondering where he had gone before she decided to follow. She held her breath and sprinted across the scrubby sand to the cliff, throwing herself onto the ground when she reached the edge.

Below, she could see the waves splashing onto the beach, but Alex was nowhere to be seen. Hardly daring to breathe, Chastity edged closer, hanging her torso over the cliff to see better. Still, there was no one.

Then she heard the crunch of pebbles, of someone scrabbling up the steep path that led from the beach. She pulled herself up, dove away from the path, and, still lying on the sand, turned her face away from the sounds.

Let him go away, she prayed, without seeing me.

Minutes passed; she could hear his labored breathing and waited, her heart pounding so loudly, surely he could hear. She waited for another fifteen minutes, counting the seconds out with painful patience. Then, she could stand it no longer and turned her face, quickly. Her eyes scanned the nearby horizon for a figure. He was no longer there.

But was he still watching from the trees? she asked herself. Another fifteen minutes passed, and Chastity got to her feet. She had been through enough, she thought. If Alex was watching, then so be it. She had a question or two for him, too!

There was no shout of recognition or discovery, and Chastity made her way back to the woods, grumbling about lack of sleep and stupid assignations.

An hour later, she was back in the house, having rubbed down her sister's mare and checked on Baby's welfare. She entered her room and stopped, an eerie feeling creeping over her, causing goose bumps. She lighted all the candles and searched the room. Next, she checked the dressing room and peeked in on her sisters. All was as it should have been.

Bone weary, she changed her clothes and slipped between the sheets. Reaching over to extinguish the candles on the table, she caught her breath.

There, beside the candles, was the book Alex had discovered her reading that first night in the salon. He had rescued her from her mother's wrath by claiming the book as his own and pocketing it.

As though it were made of fire, Chastity reached for it and opened it. A small square of paper fell out, and she picked it up. She read:

Next time ask, if you wish to go along.

A

Chapter Five

Chastity entered the stable yard the next morning with a marshall look in her eye. She had tossed and turned again, and her mood was none too malleable. Just let him make one flippant remark, she thought contentiously.

"I was afraid you wouldn't make an appearance," he said heartily, striding across the yard.

"Now why would you think that? You, on the other hand, are ten minutes late."

"I beg your pardon," he said, sweeping an elegant bow.

Chastity gave an unladylike snort, and turned to James the groom for a hand up.

Alex cleared his throat noisily.

"Yes?" she said, looking at him haughtily.

"I believe you have my horse."

"What?" she exclaimed, haughtiness replaced by indignation.

James took a few steps back as Alex walked forward and put his hand on Baby's bridle.

"You agreed that I had won the right to ride Baby on our next outing. Did you forget?" he asked, smiling sweetly.

Chastity restrained her desire to slap the smile from

his face and merely pursed her lips. She stepped aside, granting Alex his request with an elegant wave of her hand.

"Be my guest," she said. "James, saddle Father's horse for me."

"Your father's horse? Do you think you should?" asked Alex with an innocent air.

Chastity seethed in silence, refusing to answer him.

If her silence was meant to discomfit Alex, it seemed to be having the opposite effect. He began to whistle gaily, ignoring her completely.

"Ready?" he called cheerfully.

Chastity gave him a pursed-lipped nod, applied her riding crop, and sent the gelding down the drive at a jolting trot. When they reached the lane, she kicked him without looking back and sent the beast galloping.

Alex was soon passing her by, much to her chagrin. He raised his riding crop to her in salute and pulled Baby up to remain at her side.

It was a gruelling pace, and Chastity would never knowingly mistreat her mount, so she slowed the gelding to a comfortable trot.

"More like it," said Alex, doggedly keeping to her side.

"I did it for the horses," she snapped.

"Not willing to forgive me yet?" he asked.

"I don't know what you're talking about," she said.

"Oh? Very well then, we'll simply pretend nothing happened and talk about the weather, like good English citizens. I do hope this fine weather lasts, don't you? Of course, it is frightfully unusual for this time of year. Do you think we'll have snow for Christmas?"

Chastity swallowed a chuckle and tilted her nose even higher in the air.

"Oh, I say, is that a thunderstorm coming up? I do

hope not, Miss Hartford. I should hate to see you drown," he added solicitously.

Chastity allowed a small, very small, laugh to pass her lips.

"That rather exhausts my weather talk. Let's see, what next? The latest on-dit from London?"

"As if I would care about that!"

"Aha! She speaks, yet she says nothing. Her eye discourses; I shall answer it! No, I am too bold!"

Chastity pulled her horse to a stop, and Alex did likewise.

"You are absurd," she said, but the frost was gone from her voice. *"Romeo and Juliet?* And have you cast yourself in the role of Romeo?"

"Perhaps, since you must represent the beautiful Juliet," he teased.

A shadow crossed her eyes, and she said, "You know I don't care for fulsome compliments."

"What about the truth? Do you care for that? Why did you follow me last night?"

"I saw you from my window and I . . . I wanted to know where you could be going . . . on my horse," she added.

"And did the answer satisfy you?" Alex asked, suddenly curious if she had followed him before. But how to find out without admitting he had been making regular excursions at night?

"I suppose it has to, doesn't it?" she said, looking him in the eye.

He nodded. "Come on. Let's go and purloin a coachman's whip!" he said, dismissing the subject as he sent Baby down the road at a brisk trot.

They arrived at the posting inn at Dover to find that the next coach was not expected until noon.

Alex pulled out his timepiece and said, "Well, I propose we have some refreshments. I'll get us a private

parlour while you go upstairs and do whatever it is you
ladies do."

"So considerate," she simpered.

Upstairs, Chastity stripped off her gloves and removed her hat. Her old blue riding habit was plainly
cut, but it still set her figure off admirably. She
smoothed her hair and brushed the dust from the folds
of her skirts before making her way downstairs.

She found Alex already busy with a tankard of ale,
but he had waited for her before diving into the cold
collation accompanied by hot scones, butter, and honey.
Chastity's single piece of toast for breakfast had long
since been forgotten, and she, too, heaped her plate.

When their hunger was appeased, they sat back,
looked at each other, and began to laugh.

"Was it really that good, or were we just that hungry?" Alex asked, his laughter subsiding.

"It was good, but I was also starving. I didn't realize
it until I smelled those scones."

"They were good, weren't they? I'll have to ask the
cook for the recipe. Maybe my batman can manage
them if they're not too complicated."

Chastity's smile disappeared abruptly. "Your batman?" she said anxiously, a frown wrinkling her brow.
"Are you going back to the Peninsula?"

Alex wanted to kick himself. He certainly hadn't
planned to talk about that—yet. Still, there was no
avoiding it now.

"Well, yes, if my leg continues to improve."

"Oh. I hadn't thought. Of course you would rejoin in
that case. And it has improved, hasn't it?" Chastity's
eyes demanded a truthful answer.

"Almost as good as new," he said, trying to sound
cheerful. He failed miserably, but there was nothing he
could add. He put his hand over hers, and she didn't re-
coil.

Taking a deep breath, Chastity smiled again. "What time is it?"

Relieved that she had chosen to change the subject, Alex again took out his timepiece. "Almost twelve. Now, how are we going to do this?"

"You faint, and I'll take it during the confusion," she said, managing a straight face.

"Very funny. I don't swoon either. No, I'll tell you what, since you insist on being the thief, I'll go out there looking for you. I'll act like I'm inebriated, impatient to be gone, and I'll start yelling and screaming because I can't find you anywhere."

"I can visualize that," she said primly.

"Ha, ha. Anyway, in the confusion, you take the whip, hide it . . . well, hide it somewhere, sneak around back of the building, and suddenly appear. Our horses should be ready by then, and we'll make good our escape."

"I suppose that's as good as anything. Give me a few minutes to go around the back of the inn and sneak across to the other side of the coach." They heard the noisy approach of the Mail from London.

"Good luck," he said, grinning, and kissing her hand.

"You, too," she said, blowing him a kiss as she went out the door.

Alex waited five minutes before staggering outside in his best drunken impression.

"Where's m' horse!" he said loudly.

"Right away, guvner," said an ostler.

"And m' sister's horse," he yelled after the boy. He peered around the yard in a myopic manner, his head swiveling as though it were not secured to his neck properly. "Where's m' sister?" he said quietly, looking back toward the inn where the coachmen were drinking their ale. "I said, where's m' sister?"

His voice had risen, and one of the drivers came closer, saying, "Misplaced yer sister, 'ave ye?"

"No, damn you, I haven't misplaced her. She was here a minute a . . . ago. Where'd she go? Did you see her?"

" 'Aven't seen hide ner hair of 'er. Is she pretty? I'd remember 'er if she was pretty."

"How dare you comment on my sister!" yelled Alex, really enjoying himself. "I could call you out for that!"

The other driver and several ostlers had appeared, including the one leading their horses.

" 'Ere, mister, take it easy. No need to fret. She'll turn up."

Alex whirled around, facing the coach, and put his hands to his head, tearing at his hair. He grinned at Chastity who was up on the far side of the mail coach, lifting the whip down.

"Where is she?" he wailed. "Where is she? I've got to find her! Mother was counting on me! If she's run away again . . ." He gave his audience a blind stare and made a gesture as if slitting his throat. "The last time it was the dancing master. No telling who she's taken up with now!"

Chastity exited the inn at a brisk walk.

"Come along, brother. I'm right here. Everything's going to be alright," she said, soothingly. She helped him mount before allowing the ostler to throw her into the saddle. Her face still puckered with concern, she made a gesture to signify her "brother's" madness before they kicked their horses and cantered out of the yard.

Overtaken by paroxysms of laughter, they managed to put some distance between themselves and the inn before falling from the horses, almost rolling on the ground with mirth.

"Did you see their faces when I started tearing at my hair?" asked Alex, gasping for air.

"A masterly touch!" Chastity conceded. "You played right into my hands, you poor demented fool!"

"You did get it, didn't you?" he asked, suddenly remembering their mission.

Chastity grinned, turned her back to him, and began to pull the long whip out from the top of her riding habit.

"I thought at first I wouldn't be able to mount. It was very uncomfortable!"

"But any sacrifice to win the game, eh?" he said, taking the whip from her.

Reminded of the scavenger hunt, Chastity said guiltily, "I didn't exactly follow the rules."

"What do you mean?"

"I felt so bad about just taking it. You know we'll never get it back to the poor fellow."

"So? What did you do?"

"I left some money on the seat. I wasn't really paying for the whip; I have no idea what they cost. It was just a trade."

Alex grinned. "If we can stoop low enough to steal, I guess we can stoop low enough to bend one little rule and not tell anyone."

Chastity breathed a sigh of relief. "I'm glad."

Alex helped her remount and climbed onto Baby's back. He looked her up and down and said, "Of course, I wouldn't have bent the rules at all if you'd let *me* take the whip." He kicked Baby and sent him flying down the road.

Chastity caught up when he slowed the big horse.

"You really are an awful man," she said, smiling at him.

"So they tell me," he answered, leaning over Baby to untwist the reins just as a shot rang out.

TAKE ADVANTAGE OF THIS SPECIAL OFFER, AVAILABLE *ONLY* TO ZEBRA REGENCY ROMANCE READERS.

You are a reader who enjoys the very special kind of love story that can only be found in Zebra Regency Romances. You adore the fashionable English settings, the sparkling wit, the captivating intrigue, and the heart-stirring romance that are the hallmarks of each Zebra Regency Romance novel.

Now, you can have these delightful novels delivered right to your door each month and never have to worry about missing a new book. Zebra has made arrangements through its Home Subscription Service for you to preview the three latest Zebra Regency Romances as soon as they are published.

3 **FREE** REGENCIES TO GET STARTED!

To get your subscription started, we will send your first 3 books ABSOLUTELY FREE, as our introductory gift to you. NO OBLIGATION. We're sure that you will enjoy these books so much that you will want to read more of the very best romantic fiction published today.

SUBSCRIBERS SAVE EACH MONTH

Zebra Regency Home Subscribers will save money each month as they enjoy their latest Regencies. As a subscriber you will receive the 3 newest titles to preview FREE for ten days. Each shipment will be at least a $11.97 value (publisher's price). But home subscribers will be billed only $9.90 for all three books. You'll save over $2.00 each month. Of course, if you're not satisfied with any book, just return it for full credit.

CONVENIENT HOME DELIVERY

Zebra Home Subscribers get the convenience of home delivery, with only $1.50 shipping and handling charge added to each shipment. What's more, there is no minimum number to buy and you can cancel your subscription at any time. No obligation and no questions asked.

TO GET YOUR 3 FREE BOOKS
FILL OUT AND MAIL THE COUPON BELOW

FREE BOOKS

Mail to: Zebra Regency Home Subscription Service
120 Brighton Road
P.O. Box 5214
Clifton, New Jersey 07015-5214

YES! Start my Regency Romance Home Subscription and send me my 3 FREE BOOKS as my introductory gift. Then each month, I'll receive the 3 newest Zebra Regency Romances to preview FREE for ten days. I understand that if I'm not satisfied, I may return them and owe nothing. Otherwise, I'll pay the low members' price of just $9.90 for all 3 books and save over $2.00 off the publisher's price (a $11.97 value). A $1.50 postage and handling charge is added to each shipment. I may cancel my subscription at any time and there is no minimum number to buy. In any case, the 3 FREE books are mine to keep regardless of what I decide.

NAME _____

ADDRESS _____ APT NO. _____

CITY _____ STATE _____ ZIP _____
( )

TELEPHONE _____

SIGNATURE _____ **RG1694**
                    (if under 18 parent or guardian must sign)

Terms and prices subject to change. Orders subject to acceptance by Zebra Home Subscription Service, Inc.

ZEBRA HOME SUBSCRIPTION SERVICE, INC.
120 BRIGHTON ROAD
P.O. BOX 5214
CLIFTON, NEW JERSEY 07015-5214

AFFIX
STAMP
HERE

Baby reared up, and another shot sounded. Alex slid to the ground, the sand on the road turning red with his blood.

Chastity set to work, cradling Alex's head in her lap, using the hem of her habit to stanch the flow of blood. The wound appeared slight, and remembering her own fall from a tree as a girl and the profusion of blood produced by that scratch, she remained calm.

After several minutes that seemed like an eternity, the bleeding stopped, and Alex opened his eyes.

"That's one way to get into your arms," he said weakly, trying to sit up.

Chastity ignored the quip and asked, "Are you alright?"

"I will be," he said, touching the back of his head.

"Perhaps you'd better stay still a little longer."

"No, I'm fine. Did you get a glimpse of who shot me?"

"No, I was too surprised and too busy to look about."

"Probably a poacher," he said, climbing to his feet and looking about. "I seem to have mislaid my horse."

Chastity whistled, and Baby came forward, chewing a mouthful of grass.

"Is he alright?" Alex asked.

Chastity jumped up, hurrying to her horse. "I don't know!" she said, suddenly alarmed. "I hadn't thought about that." She ran a hand down his neck and across his withers.

"Just a nick, it looks like," said Alex, taking her hand to look at the trace of red. He examined the stallion more closely and found a small scratch where he had been grazed. "I took the first one; it must have happened when he reared up. Probably saved my life," he said quietly, patting the horse gently.

"You mean you think someone was trying to shoot you? On purpose? But who would . . ."

"No, I imagine it was just a poacher. Why would anyone want to shoot me?" he said, laughing, his face hidden as he kneeled down, pretending to check the horse's legs.

Chastity bent down, too, her face alive with suspicion. "What about Sir Charles? What did you say to him? He must have been very angry."

Alex straightened and pulled Chastity upright. Genuine amusement showed on his face, and Chastity breathed a sigh of relief. It was unpleasant to think that one of their house guests might have tried to kill another.

"No, Charlie would not try to shoot me. Our quarrel was much too civilized to allow for that," he said, forgetting that he had promised to call his old friend out if he didn't keep his mouth shut. "It must have been a poacher." Alex touched the wound gingerly.

"You're in pain," said Chastity, putting one hand on his arm.

"Just a headache. Still, I think I'd like to get back. Besides, we need to get our prize hidden."

"To the devil with our prize!" objected Chastity. "We need to find the man who did this!"

"No, we don't. It was probably some poor tenant farmer who thought he saw a stag." Chastity just stared dubiously at him and refused to budge. With a painful shake of his head, Alex said, "Alright, let's look for the spent shells."

They had little difficulty locating the shells. They had come from a musket, not a fowling piece, and Alex was relieved to realize that Chastity couldn't tell the difference. He knelt down, examining the hoofprints of the would-be assassin's horse. The animal favored its right foreleg heavily. It had to have been St. Pierre. Sticking to his story that it must have been a poacher, he soon had Chastity mounted and heading toward home.

They didn't speak, and Alex took the opportunity to decide what to do next. The shots had been deliberate, of that much he felt sure. Perhaps his midnight jaunts had not gone undetected. Or perhaps his gentle probing of the "comtesse" had not been gentle enough. At any rate, his life was in danger, and so was Chastity's, when she was with him.

He glanced at her, a wave of fear washing over him. When he had been given this assignment, it had seemed more of a lark than anything. He hadn't been afraid, even when he had sneaked into the comtesse's house. But now, deep in his stomach, he felt a real fear growing. He had to keep Chastity away from him.

Why, she had followed him to the beach only last night! What if something had happened to her? He had to protect her, and if that meant destroying their new-found camaraderie, then he would do so.

"You must tell Father," she said as they dismounted.

"Don't be foolish, Chastity," he began, making himself laugh at her suggestion. He held up his hand to deter her arguments. "There's no reason for that. It's over; no one was hurt, and there's no need to get some poor devil in trouble just because of bad eyesight."

"But Father is the magistrate."

"I don't care, and that's all there is to it."

Her expression was cross, but she agreed reluctantly.

When Chastity reached her room to change, she was met by her sisters, their eyes red with weeping.

"What on earth is going on?"

"Chastity, you must help us!"

Chastity's eyes grew wide with apprehension, remembering her last conversation with her sisters. Had they managed to ruin themselves since yesterday?

"Tell me what the problem is," she said, leading them

to the bed and seating them before pulling forward the chair from the escritoire.

"It's Mama! We went to her this morning," said Tranquility.

"To tell her she had been unfair," chimed in Sincerity.

"Unfair about what?" asked Chastity. To her knowledge, her mother had never been unfair to the twins.

"About you!" they exclaimed together.

Chastity smiled at them fondly, shaking her head.

"That is very good of you, but there is nothing she can do now."

"Nonsense!" said Tranquility firmly.

"We told her she had to let you come to London with us in the spring and have another Season," said Sincerity.

"I don't think that would be wise. Besides, can you see me with all the girls being presented? I'm like an older aunt!" Chastity said, laughing. It was odd, she thought. She had often wondered whether, if she only had one more chance . . . Now, the idea was not at all appealing. The reason, of course, might be the fear of encountering more people like Sir Charles and Lady Costain, who she assumed was spreading the old rumors about her.

Chastity quieted their protests with one finger raised to her lips. "You are both very kind, thoughtful girls, though you do like to tease me too much. But the truth is, I don't wish to go. I have other plans, and they don't include going to London."

"But Chastity . . ."

"Besides, what did Mother say to your demands?"

They looked at their hands folded demurely in their laps. Chastity nodded.

"I thought as much."

"She told us we would not be allowed to come downstairs until we had come to our senses," said Tranquility, her blue eyes alight with indignation.

"She said we were . . . impudent hoydens!" exclaimed Sincerity. "And we were all that was reasonable!" she added, once again stretching the truth.

Chastity laughed. "But certainly you are impudent, though not because of this. Now, dry your tears, bathe your faces, and go and apologize to Mother. I insist."

They looked relieved and started to leave.

"Are you sure, Chastity?" said Tranquility from the doorway where she had paused to look back at her older sister, a new-found respect on her face.

Chastity blew her a kiss and said decisively, "I am positive. Now, go, and don't trouble yourselves about me. I am quite content."

The door closed behind her sisters, and she unlaced her riding boots and threw them toward the armoire. She had lied; contentment was one word that she would not use to describe her present state of mind. She was angry with Alex; she was afraid of Alex.

She had enjoyed their outing too much. Oh, it had been spoiled by the accidental shooting. But she couldn't remember having laughed so gaily before. Alex made her feel young and carefree. And hopeful.

A shiver ran up and down her spine. There had been no speaking looks, no touch, but their day had been very special. She tried to tell herself she was being foolish, but she was unsuccessful.

Chastity rang for water to bathe. Sinking into the steamy liquid, she felt a delicious sense of languor. It was four days until Christmas; five more days with Alex. She would enjoy it; she would store up memories to warm her soul if loneliness became her only companion at her cottage. Most of all, she would not take any of it too seriously.

She dressed and sat down in the window embrasure,

staring outside at the garden, her mind elsewhere. The dressing bell sounded for dinner. Having dressed already, she made her way down to the kitchen, took a carrot for Baby and a bone for Buster, and let herself outside.

Buster forgot about following her after she gave him his bone, so she made her way toward the stables alone. The yard was quiet, the grooms' work finished for the day. She slipped inside the stall, fed Baby the carrot, and petted him, inspecting his small wound. James had cleaned it and put some salve on it.

Remembering Alex's blood on the saddle, she started toward the grooms' quarters to tell James it would need cleaning. Someone was in the tackroom so she started to push open the door, until one word made her freeze.

"Spies is spies, 'enry, and that's why I got out. And yer brother should 'ave, too. Those people are mean. Ever since that comtesse female came . . ."

"I know, I know, but th' money has come in handy. And now this."

The other man grumbled something about spies again which Chastity didn't catch.

Then the groom called Henry said, "I know, but this isn't spies. This is an order; a big one. We'd be able to retire on this."

"I tell you it's too dangerous, Henry, and I'm not going to go back. I'm finished."

"But it's for the man."

"Too risky."

"He's going t' get it somewhere. Might as well make some money out of it."

"Why did he wait till th' last minute?"

"All these high and mighty guests must 'ave drunk 'im dry!" laughed the one called Henry. "Come on, James. Just one more time. Why, you could make enough t' buy that little wife o' yours a cottage by the sea."

"I don't know . . ."

"Come on, there's no spies. And that boat that exciseman's been sending out 'as a 'ole in it. It's bein' repaired in the village. I saw it today. Come on."

"I suppose it'll be alright, Henry. But just this once!"

Chastity hurried to her father's study, hoping to find him there before dinner. He needed to hear what she had heard!

Almost at the open door, she paused, once again listening. Alex was in there with her father.

"Tomorrow night, or the next, I should think," Alex was saying. "They put that boat in for repairs, so . . ."

The door closed, and she was alone in the corridor. Her mother's plaintive voice could be heard from the dining room. There must be some minor problem about dinner. Chastity retreated to the salon to wait for the other guests, her thoughts whirling in confusion.

What she had heard at the stable implicated her father in the smuggling that everyone knew went on in the district. She was not shocked by this, but she was afraid he didn't know about the spies. If there were spies.

And if there were, the comtesse was one of them. And Alex was meeting secretively with the comtesse, and now he was with her father. She tried to block out the horrible possibility that both her father and Alex knew about the spies, knew about the comtesse, were involved in some way.

What should she do?

"I'm glad to see you've joined us tonight, Chastity. You look very nice," said her mother, studying every detail of her eldest child's appearance. "I would have suggested my sapphire pendant with that gown, but the pearls are becoming, too."

Chastity tried not to gape at her mother, but she was less than successful. Her mother rarely commented on her appearance without going down her list of all that was inappropriate about it. And here she was offering compliments!

Her mother cleared her throat and said in her normal brisk tone, "I wish you would step into the kitchen and calm Cook. She is in one of her humors." ·

This translated into the understanding that her mother had said something rude to antagonize Cookie, and it would be up to Chastity to smooth things over again. Chastity nodded and left the room.

At dinner, Chastity had no place to look. Every time she lifted her green eyes, they fell on her father or Alex, and she didn't wish to think about either of them or what she had heard.

Still, she had to face the possibility that both of them knew not only about the smuggling, but the spies, as well. By the time the last course was served, she had a raging headache. Her plea to be excused was denied, and she sat at the pianoforte, her head pounding with each note she played.

When Alex walked in, he studied her rigid back and frowned. She had been quieter than usual at dinner, not saying a word that he had heard. Perhaps she was displeased with him, and if that was the case, he wanted to foster her displeasure. He had to go to the beach that night, and he didn't want her following him. If she was angry enough, she wouldn't care where he went.

He walked up to Sincerity and bowed. "May I have this dance?"

"Dance?" she said, surprised since Chastity was playing a mournful ballad. Young Lord Ravenwood, seated beside her, looked daggers at him.

"I'm sure we can persuade the musicians to strike up a suitable tune," said Alex, holding out his hand. Sincerity rose with a giggle.

Lady Hartford, catching the tail end of the conversation, called for the servants to roll up the rugs and instructed Chastity to select another song. Soon, there were four couples making use of the impromptu dance floor.

Playing one melody after another, Chastity waited for someone to rescue her. As she finished each tune, she paused; surely Alex would say something now. But he didn't. Instead, he danced with every lady present, including her mother.

Almost two hours later, the revelers declared themselves too tired to dance another step. The tea tray was called for, and Tranquility poured out, Alex on one side of her on the sofa and Ruben Oxworth on the other.

Chastity accepted her cup, looked Alex in the eye, and then deliberately passed him. She found her secluded seat on the far sofa and drank her tea in exhausted, fuming silence.

Chastity went up to her room shortly afterward. She fell onto the bed, rudely telling the maid she shared with her sisters to go away. Then she called Rosey back and apologized, allowing the girl to help her into her nightrail.

After blowing out the candles, Chastity went to the window.

She didn't care what happened to him, she told herself, swiping at a lone tear crawling down her cheek. That afternoon had obviously meant nothing to him. He had probably only come to Hartford for one reason, and the comtesse was it. Or the smuggling. Or the spying.

She ran both hands through her long curls, a sign of her confusion and exasperation. The gesture made her smile momentarily, calling to mind Alex's act of drunken insanity at the inn. The smile was replaced by pursed, angry lips.

If he was involved in smuggling or spying, she needed to tell someone. She went to the wardrobe and pulled out a black riding habit. Buttoning the last button, she paused.

But what about her father? What if he was involved? She couldn't send the militia down on his head. She had to find out first if he was in on it, too. And to do this, she had to follow Alex again.

But what if he doesn't go tonight? she asked herself. Of course he will; he always does.

Had she been speaking out loud, the bitterness would have been dripping from her tongue. As it was, it shone on her frowning face and carried her down the back stairs to the stables.

Chastity saddled her sister's mare and led her to the woods, well away from both the path that led to the beach and that which lead to the comtesse's house.

She waited for what seemed like hours, watching the fading moon travel from the horizon to just over-head. Yawning continuously, she settled against the rough bark of a tree and fell asleep. Waking with a start, Chastity saw that the moon had dipped low in the sky.

Either Alex hadn't gone anywhere, or she had missed him. Chilled and cramped, she led the mare back to its stall and rubbed it down.

Alex woke refreshed the next day, ready for the out-ing his host had planned. He was anxious to see Chastity, but also uneasy. He had done all he could to make her mad the previous evening.

When he had seen her at the stables, he had decided to walk to the smugglers' cove rather than risk her detecting him and following him. When he had come back and checked on her, she had been sound asleep. Uncomfortable, to be sure, but she had been in no danger, being only a stone's throw from the stables. He had pitched a pebble at the horse, startling it and waking Chastity. Watching from the shadows until she had gone inside the house, he had finally made his way to bed.

But this morning, he didn't know if he would be greeted with disdain or melancholy. Haughtiness would be much easier to deal with, he thought, even though he was well aware he had hurt her with his callous behavior.

They were going to Dover to take a ride along the coastline on the yacht of a Lord Petersham. Lord Hartford had arranged it, telling Alex confidentially that it would give him an opportunity to study the smugglers' cove from the water.

They met on the front steps at ten sharp. Alex felt a pang of guilt when he saw Chastity, her eyes hollow from her long night.

She was dressed in a yellow gown of wool crepe. Her bonnet was fashioned out of the same material and was tied with a wide satin ribbon. Despite her air of fatigue, she looked beautiful.

Alex steeled himself against such thoughts. "Good morning," he said impersonally. He kept telling himself it was for her safety that he must treat her so.

Chastity's nostrils flared slightly; she looked as if she'd just taken a bite of soured cream. "Fitzsimmons," she said with a curt nod before turning to her father.

"May I ride in your curricle, Papa?"

"Well, I did ask Alex ..."

Alex said hastily, "I'm sure I can find another spot, my lord."

"Beside me, Mr. Fitzsimmons," gushed Tranquility, taking his arm. Ruben Oxworth, who had been by her side, followed along like an obedient puppy.

When she had her father alone, Chastity said, "Did you know I will be five and twenty in only six months?"

He smiled down at her indulgently. "I do seem to recall that."

"I will come into that inheritance from Great Aunt Sylvia."

"That's quite true."

"I have also been saving my pin money for some time, Papa."

"How very frugal of you, to be sure. What do you plan to buy? A curricle and pair, perhaps?" he teased.

"No, a house." Though his eyes never left the road, his amazement was evident, and Chastity explained, "A cottage, to be more precise. Something small and cozy. Perhaps by the sea."

He slowed the team to a restless walk, took the ribbons in one hand, and really looked at her for the first time in years. He calmed her nervous hands with his.

"I'm sorry, Chastity. I didn't realize you'd been so unhappy."

Chastity took a deep breath, and tears stung her eyes. She'd been unprepared for such instant, complete understanding.

"It hasn't been so bad, Papa. I always had you."

"Yes, but I spend far too much time in London. Maybe you could go with me from now on," he offered, wondering how he could manage to enjoy his time with his mistress with a daughter in tow.

"I don't want to go to London, Papa, except perhaps to visit all those sights Mother thought were of no interest," she said, a smile breaking forth.

"I would be delighted to show you the sights."

"Thank you. But I still want to buy my cottage. I'll have a garden, and Buster, and maybe a cat or two."

"You know, Chastity, there is more."

"No," she said quickly, shaking her head. "Don't tell me that. I've resigned myself to certain facts. But I could be happy on my own, being my own mistress. I couldn't live extravagantly, but I . . ."

"You're hardly a pauper!"

"I know, but the annuity isn't large."

"I'm not talking about that pittance my aunt left each of you girls. I'm talking about your money from me. Did you think I wouldn't settle anything on you?" Chastity stared at him, wide-eyed. "Well, did you?" he demanded.

"I hadn't thought. I mean, a dowry, yes, but I'm not marrying."

Lord Hartford permitted himself a hoot of laughter. "So you keep telling me. To begin with, I'll give you the dowry, if you're sure you'll not be marrying," he said, winking at her and causing her utter confusion.

"That would be nice, Papa," she said, placating him.

"And as for your cottage, buy it if you wish, but you'll be back at Hartford one of these days."

She shook her head. "I don't think so."

"Then who will get it when I'm gone, my girl? I have no sons, and you're the eldest. Hartford is yours, Chastity. It always has been. It's not entailed; the title dies with me. Everything—except your sisters' dowries—everything is yours."

Chastity hugged his neck, causing him to protest with a big smile on his face.

"I say, Lord Hartford! Is everything alright? Lady Hartford sent me back to see what's keeping you," called Lord Ravenwood.

"Tell her ladyship we're fine. We'll catch up."

They drove the remainder of the way with Chastity's hand tucked firmly in the crook of her father's arm. Navigating was a bit difficult, but neither one seemed to care.

The cavalcade stopped at the docks, and the party went on board, greeted by Lord and Lady Petersham, an elderly couple with perpetual smiles on their faces. Chastity knew they were both charming and intelligent, but their expressions made them appear as simpletons. They welcomed their guests with unquestionable pleasure.

Alex was amazed at the change the short ride had wrought in Chastity. She was smiling and animated, her fatigue a thing of the past. They had luncheon on deck under a brightly-striped canopy. Champagne was consumed freely, and it was a jolly assembly that sailed along the coast.

Lord Petersham took Alex, Ruben, and Lord Hartford on a tour of his little toy, as he called it. The yacht was a unique vessel. Lord Petersham had been intrigued by the steam-powered boats being tested on the Clyde River in Scotland. After extensive study, he had ordered a steam engine installed in his yacht, though it also had the traditional sails. One other source of pride for Lord Petersham was a six-pound cannon he had mounted on the bow of the yacht. It was one that had been used at the Battle of Trafalgar in 1805 when Lord Petersham had been serving as an officer in His Majesty's Navy.

When the tour was finished, the other men rejoined the ladies, but Alex stood alone at the rail. He recognized the pebbly beach where he and Chastity had walked and fought. Beyond the distant trees, he could make out the top of the house.

"You're very quiet," said Chastity, startling him.

"And you're very happy. What's the occasion?" he responded with an air of disinterest.

Chastity stiffened at his languid tone, but she said, "I spoke to my father about my desire to set up my own establishment. He thought it was a good idea and even offered to help me." She had been about to tell him she'd just discovered she was an heiress, but it was not a topic one discussed with eligible bachelors. He might think it was a hint, and she certainly didn't want that!

"A rather strange ambition for a young lady," he said. He had no trouble sounding mildly irritated. Why was she making such outlandish plans? Hadn't she realized he . . . No, of course she hadn't, especially since he was being so cold to her now. He could tell her his plans, he thought, and that would change her idea of setting up on her own.

But Chastity had digested his comment and turned a blazing gaze on him. "So much for your saying you understood my wanting to be free, to be my own mistress. You know, I thought you had changed in the last ten years. I was wrong. You are still the supremely selfish . . ."

She perceived he was paying absolutely no attention to her; he was studying the coastline intently. Chastity fell into a furious silence, recognizing the comtesse's house in the distance. It was almost obscured by the trees, well back from the cliffs, but there was no mistaking it. Below was the cove where Alex had gone the night he discovered she had followed him.

If she had been one of her sisters, she would have stamped her foot and thrown a tantrum. Instead, Chastity stalked away, going below to get away from everyone—especially Alex Fitzsimmons.

She discovered a masculine sitting area, richly decorated with sailing pictures, polished wood, and leather. She studied each painting, pausing in front of one that portrayed a tiny sailboat with a lone boy on board.

"That was my first boat. That's when I learned to

love sailing," said Lord Petersham at her elbow, his chest puffing out at the memory. "I beat every other boy in the village when we had races. What fun it was! When I went away to school, I wanted to take it with me. When my father told me there was nowhere to sail at Eton, I went on a hunger strike and refused to go." He patted his huge stomach, and Chastity laughed. "Hard to believe that now!" he added, laughing also.

"I hope I'm not intruding down here," she said.

" 'Course not, m' dear. I only came below to fetch Lady Petersham's handkerchief. You make yourself at home. I can give you a tour, if you like."

"Thank you, but I think I'll just stay here for a while. It's such a pleasant room."

"My favorite," he said, excusing himself and going back on board.

Chastity did not make herself "at home." Instead, she remained where she was, studying the painting. The scenery looked remarkably familiar. Then she saw it, the distant house on the cliffs. It was the comtesse's house, the one that had so captured Alex's attention that he had forgotten her very existence.

It was then that Chastity formed a resolution. No matter what Alex was doing with the comtesse—having an affair, or spying for the French—she would know the truth!

Chapter Six

The exhausted members of the house party returned to Hartford House late that night. The combination of sea air and sunshine that was so invigorating during their voyage had taken its toll, and most of them went straight to their chambers. Chastity watched Alex climb the stairs with a sneer of cynicism.

She was afraid she had been too obvious the night before, so she decided to precede Alex to the cliffs overlooking the beach. For the first time on her late night jaunts, she felt uneasy saddling the mare and riding alone through the woods.

Looking over her shoulder constantly, she tried to scoff at the colony of butterflies that had taken up residence in her stomach, but it was impossible. It was just all that talk of spies that had overset her, she told herself firmly. But in the next moment, she was stopping, listening, wondering.

Chastity arrived at the edge of the tree line and tethered the horse well away from the cliffs that overlooked the smugglers' cove. She walked the rest of the way, her imagination seeing mysterious figures behind every tree.

She set up watch; though what she was hoping for, she wasn't sure. If Alex showed up, it meant he was spying instead of philandering with the comtesse. If he didn't show up, it meant he was either fast asleep in a comfortable bed (a despicable act, to her way of thinking), or he had gone to the comtesse's house and was probably in her bed (a possibility that she found even more disturbing).

After this bout of rational thinking, Chastity asked herself why she should concern herself with Alex's affairs of the heart. She closed her weary eyes and shuddered. Why had he ever come back to Folkestone? If he had only stayed away, she would be happier than she had ever been. And why shouldn't she be? She was an heiress, and she was about to escape the jurisdiction of her autocratic mother. She should be deliriously happy!

And she would be, she admitted, if she hadn't fallen hopelessly, head over ears in love with Alex Fitzsimmons.

You must have a death wish, Alex told himself as he entered the comtesse's house once again. He was stretching his run of luck!

Still, he felt sure that there had to be an entrance to the cave through one of the secret passages. He recalled having discovered a passage that led directly to the basement, the logical place for a passageway to the caves to begin. But he had only found it once; it had been dark and scary, even for a brave youth of twelve or thirteen, and he had never ventured back down. Now, some eighteen years later, he couldn't remember where he had begun.

This was his third time inside the old house, and he had quickly discovered that its occupants lived in only a few rooms. Two of these, the comtesse's dressing room and the salon, were connected by the intricate hidden passageways behind the walls. The house, his godfather had told him, had been a hiding place for priests trying to escape to France during the cleansing. The passage-ways had been constructed by adding false walls throughout the house.

Alex made a quick inspection of the study before moving on to the salon, looking for some kind of communique. There was nothing. He was on his way back to the study when he heard voices coming from the kitchen areas. He shuttered his lantern and glanced outside. That was the first place they would search. He turned and slipped inside the secret passageway beside the fireplace.

"I tell you I heard something," said the comtesse, coming closer to the study.

"You are always hearing something," grumbled the crumpled Jean-Jacques.

"Shut up, you fool!"

Still muttering under his breath, Jean-Jacques threw open the door, holding the candelabra high, inspecting the room.

"I told you there was no one here," said the servant triumphantly.

The comtesse stepped into the room, her aristocratic nose in the air. "He was here, I tell you. Smell."

"I am not a dog," said Jean-Jacques derisively.

"No, you are not that intelligent! Can you not smell the smoke from a lantern?"

Jean-Jacques sniffed obediently and shook his head. "It is from our candles," he protested.

"Fool!" snapped the comtesse.

After a detailed inspection of the room, during which Alex held his breath, the comtesse turned back to the servant and said, "Be ready to leave soon. Tell Remi to prepare for our departure. I don't like it here anymore; I think my masquerade has been penetrated. After the shipment is unloaded, we will return to France on the boat."

"He won't like it," said Jean-Jacques.

"I don't care; I'm not going to ask for his blessing!"

Frustrated from another futile watch, Chastity went downstairs early for breakfast. Her father was there before her, and she greeted him warmly. After a quick good morning, he returned to his newspaper.

"Papa," said Chastity, munching thoughtfully on a piece of toast.

"Hm?"

"Are the wine cellars low?"

Lord Hartford frowned behind his paper before lowering it slowly. "What would make you ask that?"

"I was just wondering. Mama has been serving a great deal of champagne and such," said Chastity, feeling horrible about the lie.

Hartford rose, leaving a half-eaten steak on his plate. "I assure you we are in no danger of running dry; I have ordered a large shipment," he said, causing Chastity's heart to beat in an extraordinary manner. "I hadn't realized you were so attached to spirits," he teased.

"You know I am not. Oh, by the way, has Mr. Fitzsimmons been down? We had plans to continue our search for the scavenger hunt," she said, the lies rolling off her tongue more easily each time, she thought.

"This morning? Funny, he didn't mention it. He said something about riding to Folkestone."

"Oh, he must have forgotten. At least that will give me a chance to finish the reticule I'm knitting for Sincerity's Christmas present," she said, knowing she had no intention of sitting calmly in her room while Alex went out on his secret rendezvous.

"Well, have a pleasant day, my dear," said her father.

"Thank you, Papa."

As soon as he had left the room, Chastity abandoned her toast and tea and headed for her room. Changing quickly into a blue habit with a froth of lace at the neck, she gave herself only a cursory inspection in the mirror and hurried to the stables.

At least, she thought dryly as she watched James throw the sidesaddle on Baby, she would have the use of her own horse. The groom cupped his hands to throw her into the saddle. As Chastity grabbed the pommel, the saddle slipped, turning sideways.

"James! Didn't you tighten the girth?"

"I'm sorry, Miss Hartford. I forgot how he always blows up his stomach. I'll tighten it right now."

She watched the groom's jerky movements as he performed his simple task.

"Is something wrong, James?" she asked solicitously, afraid she knew only too well what was troubling him.

"Nothing, miss," he said, stepping back. "There, that should do the trick." He helped her into the saddle without any mishap this time.

"Thank you," said Chastity. "By the way, how is Jane?"

"She's fine, miss. We, uh, we want to thank you for the basket," he said, his halting words showing Chastity how difficult it had been for him to accept the small gift.

"You know your mother-in-law, James. She loves to bake," she said, hoping to salve his pride. "And we all love to eat her cakes and biscuits," she added.

"That's a fact, miss," he said with a smile.

"James," she began, leaning down so no one else could hear them, "you must send for me when it is Jane's time. I want to help."

"I'll let you know," he mumbled, clearing discomfited by her request. "Thank you, miss."

Chastity smiled and said good-bye. As she rode away, she was filled with bitterness. Why had Alex ever come to Folkestone? There had been no trouble with spies and such before he came, she thought mendaciously. Not that she was certain he had anything to do with it; all she felt sure about was that Alex was having an affair with the comtesse who was, in all likelihood, a French spy.

And because of all this, a fine man and his family were going to be hurt. If anything happened to James, Jane and Cook would be hurt. Chastity's expression became set and she promised herself she would do anything to stop the "shipment" before any of the locals could be dragged into danger.

The distance to Folkestone was not long when riding Baby, and she had little trouble locating Alex. Perplexed, she watched as he left the old building where Lieutenant Humphries lodged, seen out by the lieutenant himself. My God, she thought, was the militia involved in smuggling, too?

Leaving her horse at the coaching inn, Chastity followed Alex on foot, his path leading him to the beach. He paused beside an old fisherman who was carving a miniature boat. Chastity watched from the Strand, not daring to venture any closer. How she wished she could hear what he was saying.

After a few minutes, Alex walked with the old man to the boats and boarded one. He reappeared shortly, whistling softly and now in possession of a large package. Puzzled, she followed him to his next destination, Folkestone's only jewelry shop, which also sold navigational instruments. Creeping close enough to peek in the window, Chastity watched him by-pass the nautical section; the shop owner bowed and scraped as he produced a velvet display of jewelry. Chastity fumed in silence.

Alex left Folkestone, heading back for Hartford House. Chastity trailed him at a safe distance. He turned off the road after passing the comtesse's house and entered the woods. She followed cautiously, wishing with all her heart things had worked out differently.

She watched him, seated on his horse, leaning on the pommel, gazing at the run-down mansion. Mooning over the comtesse, she thought. Perhaps things were not so rosy for Alex; not that *she* hoped to gain from such a situation.

Still, the sight of Alex gazing forlornly at the comtesse's abode was more than she could stand. She turned Baby toward home.

Chastity hadn't gone far when she heard a shot ring out. It had come from Alex's direction, and she turned the stallion and headed back toward the comtesse's at a canter. Alex had gone. She stood up in the saddle and surveyed the area, but he was no longer there.

Puzzled, she continued on her way home.

Alex rode out from his hiding place. He, too, searched the area with his eyes, but his quarry had also disappeared, probably frightened off by Chastity's approach.

It had been the gatekeeper, he felt certain. That's what he deserved for riding so close in daylight, he told himself.

And why? He had accomplished nothing, short of being shot at. There was no doubt about it, he had to quit thinking about Chastity. He had known she was following him, and he had wanted to tease her, make her jealous by acting lovesick over the comtesse.

Instead, he had put himself and her in danger. From now on, he would take his assignment more seriously. Two attempts on his life were nothing to scoff at.

When Chastity rode into the stable yard, she was met by Hale, the head groom, who helped her dismount.

"Where's James? Is Jane . . . ?" Chastity asked anxiously.

"No, 'e said 'e wasn't feeling too good, miss, so I sent 'im 'ome for the afternoon."

"He's sick? I hope it's nothing serious," she said.

"Like as not, miss, it's just worry. 'E's been that nervous lately."

Chastity nodded, a frown creasing her forehead. Things were worse than she feared. Here she was, with knowledge in hand about the smugglers, and no place to turn. She had thought to speak to Lieutenant Humphries until she had seen him shaking Alex's hand. Any other time, she would have consulted her father, but he, too, was involved in some way—not spying, to be sure, but certainly at one end of the smuggling.

Helpless and worried, she retreated to her room, spending the remainder of the afternoon at the window watching the stables in case Alex should decide to make a move.

Dinner, as usual, was for Chastity a silent affair. Afterward, she played the pianoforte until the gentlemen joined the ladies. Rising from the bench, she planned to retire, not caring what her mother might say or think.

But Alex caught her up in the corridor.

"Chastity, a word with you, please," he said, giving her his most disarming smile.

Chastity held herself erect, preceding him into the smaller receiving room.

"I've got something to show you," he said, going over to the sofa and pulling out a package from behind it.

"I'm sure I have no desire to see . . ." But she did, for she recognized the packet he had received on the old fisherman's boat, and her curiosity got the best of her.

"It's the net," he said proudly. "I'm afraid I broke the rules again. I told him he'd find a new net waiting for him at one of the shops in town. He was quite pleased with the bargain."

Tears filled Chastity's eyes, and she forced them away. What was he doing to her? One minute she was certain he was in league with the spies and smugglers, and the next, he was pulling out some ridiculous scavenger hunt prize.

"Chastity! Is something wrong?" he asked, incredulous at her reaction.

Chastity sniffed loudly, wiped her eyes, and said gruffly, "Definitely not! I merely have something in my eye!" She looked around wildly, glancing up. "I always get teary when I'm around mistletoe," she lied. Alex took her hand, and she wrenched it free, saying, "No! Not again!"

He backed away, his hazel eyes dark with wrath. "You needn't have worried. I was only going to lead you away from the mistletoe! I wouldn't dream of kissing you."

"Oh," she said, feeling extremely foolish, and angry with him for making her feel that way.

Alex stepped into the hall and turned back to say coldly, "Perhaps we should go ahead and show the others what we have found for the scavenger hunt. That way we can put an end to this farce of a partnership."

"Fine," she snapped, throwing her head back defiantly. "I'll go and get the rest of the things!"

"Good!"

Chastity let her anger carry her up the stairs to her room. Opening the armoire, she reached far inside to pull out the whip, doll, snuffbox, seashell, and the parrot's feather she had retrieved from a trunk in the attic, before she had to dash away the tears. Tears of anger, she tried to tell herself.

Downstairs, she burst into the salon, drawing her mother's reprimand down on her head.

"Sorry, Mother, my hands were full," she said curtly.

Her mother gaped at her, astonished by her daughter's tartness. Chastity met her gaze with the wide, innocent stare that never failed to infuriate her mother.

"Chastity—" began Lady Hartford.

"Well, let's see what they've found," said her father, stepping between them for the first time in Chastity's life. He picked up each item in turn, commenting on it, looking from Alex who was as rigid as stone, to Chastity, whose eyes were wild with fury. When Lord Hartford had finished, he turned to the other guests and said, "Not bad. They've come up with five of the items; has anyone else done as well?"

"No," said a petulant Sincerity.

"But we will!" boasted Lord Ravenwood.

"I certainly won't beat them," lamented Lady Costain, "since my partner found it necessary to leave so suddenly."

Lady Hartford almost smiled again.

"What a bunch of lazy people you are!" said old Lady Ravenwood, causing a stir among the rest of the assembled party. "Why, in my day, we would have found everything on the list a week ago!"

"Now, Grandmamma," began her grandson, a blush spreading across his fair features. "You mustn't . . ."

"Don't tell me what I mustn't! I'm almost eighty years old; I'll do and say anything I please!" She got to her feet and snapped at Chastity, "Don't just stand there. Help me to my room, girl!"

Chastity complied with alacrity. What a chance to escape! Ordered to leave by the old tartar herself! Her mother couldn't complain about that!

Once out of earshot, though, she felt less fortunate.

"So, have you brought him up to scratch yet? I noticed the two of you leaving together. A little kiss under the mistletoe?" asked the old lady eagerly.

This was so far from the truth, Chastity laughed out loud, the sound harsh even to her own ears.

"No, my lady, I'm afraid there's no hope in that direction. Mr. Fitzsimmons and I would not suit!"

"Stuff and nonsense! If ever two people would suit, it's the two of you. I've seen the way you look at your mother; you're a saucy chit and that's just what Fitzsimmons likes. And he looks at you, too, at dinner. He may not talk to me, but I watch him, and he looks at you every chance he gets."

Chastity shook her head, willing herself not to cry again. "No, my lady, I think this time you are mistaken. Mr. Fitzsimmons and I do not even like each other." Though this was untrue, at least on her part, she felt no compunction about lying.

Lady Ravenwood cocked her head doubtfully, but she nodded finally. Poking Chastity with a bony finger, she cackled, "I'll find you a beau! You come to London in the spring with those namby-pamby sisters of yours, and I'll find you a real man!" With this, her ladyship entered her room, ordering her maid to close the door on Chastity.

Chastity's next destination was her room, but she was not to find peace there. Her mother awaited her.

"Chastity, I'll not have you speaking to me in front of others in such a disrespectful manner! You were not raised to be impudent. I don't know where it comes from!"

"Perhaps, Mother, it comes from knowing that no matter what I do, you will always find fault with it. Therefore, over the years, I have found it much more efficacious to either avoid your company or to obey blindly. But tonight, I had neither the desire nor patience to humor you."

"How dare you! I'll lock you in your room and put you on bread and water!"

"No, you won't. Those days are gone, and soon I'll be gone, too."

"Chastity!"

Dispassionately, Chastity looked down at her mother, who had seated herself abruptly on the bed. "Tell me, Mother, how is it I was never told that I would inherit Hartford House?"

"Why, I . . . that is, your father and I didn't want to show any favoritism to you over your sisters."

Chastity gave a sniff of disbelief. "Oh, you managed that nicely. It came as quite a shock the other day when Papa told me. He thought I knew."

"It would have puffed you up, made you conceited."

"Rubbish," said Chastity succinctly. "Oh, I don't blame you alone. Papa could have told me, should have told me. But that's neither here nor there."

"Chastity," said her mother quietly, her tone earning Chastity's attention. "It is difficult to have a daughter so very different from oneself, so intimidating."

Chastity noted there were no tears in her mother's eyes, but there was an air of apology in her mien. She surmised it was the closest to an apology her mother would get; she listened.

"I wanted very much for you to be a boy so your father would have his heir, and I wouldn't have to . . . but you were not. Not physically. But you were never the angelic little doll that I could dress up and show off. Just when I would tell the nurse to bring you in to show you to guests, you would come romping into the room with a torn apron and bare, muddy feet!" Even after all those years, Lady Hartford's memories raised her voice in resentment at that innocent child. "You always disagreed with me when I told you what to wear; you would look up at me with those shocking green eyes and say 'no'."

"Mother, surely you don't hold that against me still," said Chastity.

"No, no, but there were other things. You grew up; you looked like your father's mother, not me. You're tall, graceful. You liked riding and fishing. And by that time, the twins had arrived, and I had two dolls to play with. And they were so like me," she added with passion before falling silent.

Chastity heaved a sigh, her pain explained, and somehow lessened.

"I don't hate you, Chastity. I simply don't understand you," said her mother, looking up at her daughter with a puzzled frown on her face.

Chastity said quietly, "I never thought you hated me, Mother. Nor do I hate you. But I am going to set up my own establishment as soon as may be. I think it would be best for both of us."

Her mother considered this for a moment before nodding. "You are probably right," she said, adding with a smile. "As usual."

"Good night, Mother."

"Good night, Chastity."

The door closed after her mother, and Chastity fell on the bed, not weeping, but thoughtful, wishing things could have been different. After a five minute bout of self-pity, she forced herself to sit up and return to the present.

Things were looking better, she told herself. With her father's help, she could begin looking for a suitable cottage almost immediately. Then she could take one of the maids from the kitchens as a cook, and hire James to look after Baby and the pair she meant to purchase.

Chastity paused in her ruminations. What was she thinking? James might not live to be hired by her. He was probably off right now getting captured or, worse yet, shot as a smuggler! And Jane and her baby . . .

Chastity changed rapidly to a dark habit and hurried

down to the stables. She paused in front of the tack room where a light burned.

"James? What on earth are you doing here at this time of night?"

He grinned and held up the bridle he was polishing. "I got t' feeling right hearty again, miss, so I came back t' finish my work. I don't want t' lose this position!"

Chastity gave him a wide smile. "You needn't worry about that, James. You'll always have a position at Hartford."

"Thank you, miss."

"Has there been anyone else down here?" she asked casually.

"No, only Mr. Hale stopped by to check on the light, just like you."

"Oh, well, good night."

"Good night, miss," he said, beginning to whistle.

Chastity went down the row of stalls; then she walked across the small paddock to Baby's stall. Not surprisingly, the stallion was gone. Chastity swallowed a sinking feeling. She had missed him. There was no use trying to follow him now. And hopefully, since James was still working, the "shipment" was not arriving that night. With great weariness, Chastity returned to her room to get the best night's sleep she had had in almost a week.

Chastity found herself much sought after the next day. Her plans to keep Alex within her sight were thwarted from the start. Coming down to the breakfast room, she was waylaid by her sisters, who dragged her back upstairs to help them select gowns and bonnets for their picnic with Lord Ravenwood and Ruben Oxworth.

An hour later, when they were finally dressing and

she could escape, Chastity was captured by Ruben, who looked around surreptitiously before ushering her into a little-used morning room.

"It is only two days until Christmas, Miss Chastity," he began, sitting down and then rising and taking a quick turn around the small room.

"That is true, Mr. Oxworth," she said, hiding her impatience.

"I need your advice."

She waited for him to continue, and when he did not, Chastity asked, "About what?"

"I shouldn't even be considering . . . I am far too old . . ."

"You are hardly in your dotage," consoled Chastity with a smile of encouragement. She thought she knew where this was leading, but she was fearful it meant only heartbreak for Mr. Oxworth.

"No, I'm not, am I? I am really quite fit. I sit a horse well, and I know that sort of thing matters to you young ladies."

Chastity thought silently that such a thing wouldn't make any difference if the heart were engaged.

"I was thinking I might buy your mother a little something, you know, to sort of win her over," he finished in a rush, sitting down in front of her and peering fiercely into her eyes.

Chastity swallowed her surprise and asked simply, "My mother?"

"Yes, I . . ." Ruben seemed to discover a joke and said, laughing, "No, no, I don't wish to win your mother over in that way! But I know she would not approve of my giving Tranquility my mother's pearls."

"Your mother's pearls?" echoed Chastity, clearly puzzled.

Ruben sighed and said, "I fear I've gone about explaining this in a rather backward manner. I am in love with Tranquility. Though I don't want to ask for her hand until after she has had her Season, I do want to give her a token, a symbol, if you will, of my devotion. At first I thought to buy her a piece of jewelry, but I was afraid that would never be acceptable to your mother. But I thought that if it was something I already owned, then it might be alright."

"But pearls are too expensive, Mr. Oxworth. Mother would never approve, especially if they are a family heirloom."

Ruben sat back gloomily. "Perhaps this is all wrong. What do you think, Miss Chastity? Have I a prayer with Tranquility?"

Chastity could not find it in her heart to give him false hope, so she said, "Tranquility is very young; you must give her time. I think she is quite attached to you, but you mustn't rush her."

"I know, I know. I preach patience to myself, but when I am with her ... Do you know, I am seven and forty, and I have never been in love before. It is the most uplifting and most depressing state in the world."

"I know," said Chastity quietly.

Ruben patted her hand and said bracingly, "Never fear, we shall come about. Just you wait and see."

Chastity forced a smile for him. "I'll tell you what to do, Ruben. Buy Tranquility a music box; she loves them."

"Really? Do you think I can find one in Folkestone, or should I ride to Dover?"

"There are some at the jewelry shop in Folkestone," said Chastity. "But you must buy two; one for Tranquility and one for Sincerity. That way, Mother will not refuse."

"Of course! I should have thought of that myself! I'll leave right after I get back from the picnic."

"Good luck, Ruben," she said.

He turned and smiled back at her, his face glowing. "Thank you, Chastity. Thank you for your help and for listening without laughing."

"As if I would!" she said, returning his smile.

Chastity left the morning room, cautiously peering into the corridor before heading for the kitchens and freedom. But once again, her luck was quite out.

"Chastity!"

Chastity cringed at the sound of her mother's plaintive voice. "Yes, Mother?"

"Could you please help me with this menu?"

Chastity's brows rose in surprise. It was the most civil request she could ever recall hearing her mother make.

"What is the matter, Mother?" she asked, walking to the table where Cook and Lady Hartford sat poring over recipes and lists.

"We want something grand for Christmas Day, but it is tradition that we give the afternoon off to the staff."

"I told you, my lady, my girls and I are willing to do what is necessary. It's not every year we've got a house full of gentry visiting for Christmas," said Cook.

"I know, but it is tradition," said Lady Hartford.

"Why not have two dinners," said Chastity. Both older women looked at her as if she had lost her mind. She held up a hand and said, "Cooking two goose dinners with all the trimmings shouldn't be any more difficult than cooking one. Hire extra girls from the village for tomorrow so that most of the work is done then. On Christmas Day, we will have our feast in the dining hall, set out in a most continental manner, *au buffet*. Here, in the kitchens, the servants, and their families, can do the same."

Lady Hartford and Cook frowned, looking at each other. Finally, Lady Hartford said, "It might work."

Cook nodded and said thoughtfully, "Yes, if th' families were included. And I think my sister and nieces might be willing to help tomorrow if they were invited for Christmas dinner the next day."

"Then by all means, Cook, please go and see them," said Lady Hartford, with rare tact. "They would be well-paid, also," she added.

This seemed to decide it for Cook, for she rose with surprising grace for one her size and said, "Yes, my lady. I'll have James drive me over in the cart immediately." She turned to Chastity and smiled, "Thank you, miss. That was a good idea you had."

Alone with her mother, Chastity rose to leave. "Cook was right, Chastity," her mother said. "I appreciate your solution. Thank you."

"I'm glad I was able to help, Mother," she said, giving her a slight smile.

Things appeared to be changing, and Chastity was glad, but she was also cautious. All her life, her mother had treated her one way; she could not help but doubt a complete reversal in attitude overnight. Nevertheless, she told herself, it was Christmas, and she was glad there was peace between her and her mother.

Chastity's mood turned when she was greeted at the stables with the news that Mr. Fitzsimmons had ridden out early that morning and had said he would be gone all day. Frustrated, she called Buster to heel and went for a walk.

Alex arrived in Dover before eleven o'clock and went straight to the docks. He was welcomed by the smiling Lord Petersham, alone this time.

"Well, my boy, are the plans all set?" asked his lordship, rubbing his plump hands together in anticipation when they had been served refreshments in the cozy sitting room below decks.

"Yes, Humphries will cover both ends. I appreciate your help."

Lord Petersham shook off his praise, saying, "Think nothing of it. Glad to help! Why, I was with Nelson, you know!"

"Yes, I was told that. It must have been quite a row," Alex said, knowing the comment would send the former sailor on a long series of reminiscences, but quite willing to indulge him.

Finally, Lord Petersham wound down. After sitting thoughtfully for a minute, he asked about the project at hand.

Alex related the rest of the details quickly before saying good-bye and turning his horse back to Folkestone. He ate a quick luncheon at the posting inn before returning to the jewelry shop he had visited the day before. The owner brought out a velvet box, opening it with a flourish.

"Very nice, just what I had in mind. You are truly an artist, sir," said Alex, smiling and holding the delicate gold pendant up so it caught the light.

"Thank you, Mr. Fitzsimmons. I'll just wrap it up for you," said the jeweler, pleased by the words of praise.

Alex wandered around the shop, picking up a spyglass, looking through a sextant.

"Surprised to find you here, Fitzsimmons," said Ruben Oxworth, entering the shop and stopping.

"Might say the same about you, Oxworth," he replied.

"Oh, I'm just doing a bit of Christmas shopping. Thought there might be something in here that would be suitable.

"Something for Miss Tranquility," said Alex with a grin.

Ruben blushed beneath his weathered skin. "Perhaps,

and Miss Sincerity, too. Wouldn't do to neglect one of the girls."

"Then you'll be buying three," said Alex, continually amazed how people overlooked Chastity's existence.

Ruben was clearly surprised by his observation. "Why, I hadn't thought about Miss Chastity. Of course I must get something for her as well. I wonder if she would like a music box, too?"

"Will there be anything else, Mr. Fitzsimmons?" asked the shop owner, returning with Alex's small package.

Ruben commented, "Looks like you need to do a bit more shopping, too. Surely there's not something for Tranquility and Sincerity in that little package, too?"

Alex grimaced, wondering how Oxworth, with whom he had shared almost no conversation, had guessed the package was for Chastity. Had he been so transparent?

Gruffly, he replied, "Some of us don't care about the little niceties. I give presents when and to whom I please."

"No need to rip up at me, Fitzsimmons. You've my blessings. Miss Chastity is a treasure; you'll be lucky to win her," said Ruben. It was obvious he wasn't sure Alex was good enough for Chastity.

"Couldn't agree more," said Alex, pocketing the package. "See you back at Hartford House, Oxworth. There's a ball or something tonight, isn't there?"

Ruben nodded. "Good-bye."

When Alex had gone, Ruben asked the shop owner to divulge the contents of Alex's package.

"That is confidential, sir. Mr. Fitzsimmons had me design something special."

"You can tell me," said Ruben, holding out a gold sovereign which the shop owner took before leaning over the counter to whisper in Ruben's ear.

* * *

Alex finished with his various projects and turned his horse toward Hartford House, traveling along the beach. He paused at the path that led up to the house, unwilling to return to the inactivity promised by the afternoon before a ball. All the ladies would be resting, and the gentlemen would be engaged in desultory conversation, cards, or perhaps billiards.

Alex continued along the beach instead, the cliffs gradually descending to sea level. He dismounted, leaving his horse to crop the scrubby grass while he walked. Shoving his hands into his pockets, he grimaced.

Chastity. He wondered if he could stay aloof until his business was accomplished. Every time he met Chastity, he wanted to take her in his arms and declare his love. Instead, he had to keep up the pretense of dislike and stir up the fires of discord.

He smiled, remembering her behavior the previous evening under the mistletoe. He had not had to pretend anger then! When she had pulled away from him, he had wanted to hurt her. Never mind that he had lied when he told her he had no intention of kissing her.

Pulling the package out, he turned it this way and that. As soon as everything was over, he would give it to her. It could be his peace offering.

"A present for the comtesse?" called Chastity.

Alex looked up to watch her languid approach, bending down to pat Buster's silky head as he did. The sun caught the highlights of her shining hair, which fell unrestrained around her shoulders. Her shoes and stockings lay on the beach. With one hand, she held her skirt up to avoid the water. She looked like a sea nymph—a very tall one.

"Jealous, is she?" he whispered to the dog. "That is promising." Not for the first time, he wished he could tell Chastity the truth, but he had to wait, had to keep her at arm's length, he told himself sternly. Patience. All it wanted was a bit of patience.

She stopped in front of him, staring pointedly at the package, her haughty expression completely out of place with her bare feet. She waited for him to respond.

"For the comtesse?" he echoed with a hearty laugh. "No, it's not for her. Now, why would you think it was for the comtesse?"

"Never mind, it was only a thought," said Chastity. I hate being lied to, she thought crossly.

"Chastity," Alex said softly.

She looked up at him, her eyes wide, her heart pounding, her lips turning down at the corners in an endearing manner. Alex took her hand in his, his touch causing her to shiver. Patience, patience, his good sense cautioned. His eyes took their fill as they stood transfixed. Patience, patience. He released her hand.

"How is it you've managed to escape your mother this afternoon? I thought she would have you and your sisters resting."

Chastity tossed her head and said, "Haven't you heard? I do as I please now."

"Oh? So you've finally achieved freedom. How does it feel?"

"Wonderful, and I have no intention of ever giving it up! I am my own mistress, and I intend it to stay that way!"

Alex frowned; this was not exactly what a man wanted to hear from the woman he was going to ask to be his wife. He wouldn't mind her being independent as long as she wanted him to be her husband.

"You sound as if you plan to be a hermit," he said, trying to make light of her statement.

"Hardly, but one may participate in society without being bound by it."

"But Chastity, surely you've considered the possibility of marriage," he probed, none too subtly.

Chastity flashed him a furious glare, one brow rising dangerously. How dare he throw her past and her name in her face! Without a word, she turned on her heel and fled, calling her dog so fiercely, he left Alex's side and obeyed.

"Now you've done it," Alex said, shaking his head dolefully. But it was for the best, he told himself. If she remained angry with him, she would not follow him, and she wouldn't be hurt.

And tomorrow, or the next day, he would go to her.

Chapter Seven

Chastity was in no mood for dancing or socializing. But despite her declaration of independence, she followed her mother's dictates and dressed for the ball.

She avoided Alex by keeping to her room until the last minute. She didn't know if he would have sought her out, but she had no intention of taking that chance.

She dressed with care in the emerald green gown her mother had bade her order for the occasion. Looking in the mirror, she reflected that there was one benefit to being four and twenty and firmly on the shelf; she could wear the colors that suited her best.

Her mother had given her a family heirloom to wear, a heavy gold necklace studded with emeralds. Rosey the maid had polished it until it gleamed, and pronounced it perfect as she fastened it around Chastity's slender neck. The largest emerald fell just above the swell of her breasts, and Chastity had to admit it was becoming.

She tugged at the low-cut bodice self-consciously. Rosey tut-tutted and said, "You look fine, miss. No need to fret about that. Mr. Fitzsimmons will love it."

Chastity frowned and tossed her head. Why was it that everyone assumed she cared what Mr. Fitzsimmons thought?

Rosey stood back and studied Chastity thoughtfully.

"Your mother has never worn that one, miss. She couldn't carry it off, but you, Miss Chastity, you look grand," said the maid before hurrying off to help her sisters finish their toilettes.

Chastity went downstairs at the last minute, entering one of the carriages and taking her seat beside Lady Ravenwood, facing backward without looking at the assembly of vehicles and people gathered in the drive.

Alex watched from beside his curricle. When she had appeared in the doorway, the bright lights of the hall behind her, the soft light of the torches in front, his self-control had almost broken. She should be the one beside him, riding to the ball. He would lag behind, savoring every minute alone with her.

"Mr. Fitzsimmons, a penny for your thoughts," said Tranquility, who was waiting for him to join her.

"Nothing," he said, clenching his jaw and climbing up.

"It's a little chilly tonight," said Tranquility, sidling closer to him.

"It is December," observed Alex dryly.

Lady Hartford entered the carriage where Chastity was, and they began to pull away. After settling her skirts, she confided to the Ladies Ravenwood and Costain, "Mr. and Mrs. Harold Simpkins are the worst kind of social climbers, but their entertainments are always lavish and well-attended."

"By people like us," observed Lady Ravenwood with a cackle.

"Yes, but it is a wonder," added her mother, not hearing Lady Ravenwood's sarcasm. "Mrs. Simpkins is unexceptional, being the daughter of a minor baronet from York. But Mr. Simpkins earned his fortune on the 'Change.' It is rumored his father was a coal miner."

"A coal miner!" exclaimed Lady Costain, who had been listening with glee.

No doubt she would spread the story of poor Mr. Simpkins' humble birth throughout the assembly in minutes, thought Chastity.

Lady Ravenwood gave a snort of derision, surprising Chastity. It seemed that if someone other than she was pronouncing judgement on mankind, the offender was just being tacky.

"When you next find yourself in the company of the Beau, I wouldn't let it be known you disapprove of honest labor," said Lady Ravenwood. At her listeners' silence, she added impatiently, "Mr. Brummel's father, I believe, was a blacksmith."

Lady Hartford and Lady Costain's disclaimers fell over each other as they retracted their comments. In the gloom of the coach, Chastity smiled as Lady Ravenwood winked at her.

Chastity reflected that while she certainly did not want to become such an eccentric as Lady Ravenwood, such an opinionated busybody, her ladyship did have a knack for setting down other people. And when those people were being ill-mannered, one had to admire Lady Ravenwood, albeit grudgingly.

The Simpkins were their nearest neighbors. Their estate was farther inland and boasted a large house which was only five years old but had been built to resemble an old manor house. It even included crumbling ruins on one side to make it appear aged. It intrigued Chastity that anyone would go to such lengths to give the illusion of antiquity, but Mr. and Mrs. Simpkins were too friendly to incur disparagement from their neighbors. Chastity suspected that her mother liked them very well, though she was at pains not to show it.

"Lady Hartford! How delightful to see you! And thank you for bringing all your illustrious guests!" said Mrs. Simpkins, shaking hands with each in turn as though they were long lost friends.

Lady Ravenwood, who had been making such demo-
cratic pronouncements moments before, lifted her nose
in the air, accepting Mrs. Simpkins' toadying as her due.
Chastity shook her head.

The introductions complete, they entered the grand
ballroom, which was swatched in silver tissue and blue
silk. Even the champagne punch had been dyed a pale
blue, the effect rather distasteful to the eye. Chastity
smiled, wondering if Lady Ravenwood would continue
her defense of the Simpkins in view of such peculiarities.

Chastity allowed Lady Ravenwood to lead her to the
chaperones' chairs where many of their neighbors were
enjoying a comfortable coze while keeping one eye on
their daughters on the dance floor. Lady Ravenwood
immediately became embroiled in a discussion with
Lady Petersham and two other matrons on what color
the cream would be at supper.

Chastity pretended to listen while trying to fade into
the background. She watched Alex pass by in front of
her, his back to the chaperones' corner as he surveyed
the dancers. Was he looking for her? she wondered. Of
course not, she told herself harshly. He was no doubt
searching eagerly for the comtesse. He probably had
that jewelry in his pocket to give her while stealing a kiss
on the balcony.

Thinking of the comtesse, Chastity began to wonder
where she might be. Three sets had come and gone
since her arrival and still there was no sign of the
Frenchwoman. It was unthinkable that she would not
attend. She had attended every function since her arrival in Folkestone last summer.

Had she and Alex had a fight?

Chastity remained hidden from view amongst the
bevy of chaperones. Only two people deigned to notice
her; they were the two young ladies who had snubbed
her for being too much sought after at her mother's

Christmas ball. This time the girls made it a point to come up and speak to her, both arm in arm with their partners for the next dance.

Chastity watched them go with a smile, their tactics only amusing her. It had been her choice to remain with the chaperones, unnoticed by most of the assembly. Besides, she had sat through too many balls only tapping her foot to the music for such taunts to bother her.

Then her father appeared before her, bowing gallantly as he smiled and requested her hand for the next set forming.

"I'd love to, Papa."

"I meant to tell you how beautiful you look tonight, my dear. You should always wear green; it suits you."

"Thank you, Papa," she said, blushing despite herself. He always thought she was beautiful, she knew, but it felt good to hear it.

"Have you danced with Alex tonight?" he asked, feeling her stiffen before they were separated by the steps of the dance.

Chastity forced a smile as she took the next man's hand and curtsied. Back with her father, she tried to ignore the query, but he would not allow it.

"Well, have you?"

"No," she said shortly.

"Hasn't he asked you? I know he was looking for you earlier."

"I don't think so, Papa. I have been sitting exactly where you found me, hardly in hiding," she replied tartly.

Her father smiled and shook his head. "It is not becoming to be dishonest."

"Who's being dis . . ." Her sentence was cut short as she moved away again. She would refuse to discuss the matter further with her father; he was obviously teasing her.

Her father had evidently decided to abandon the topic also because he next asked her if she had finished her Christmas shopping.

"Yes, I have, but I am not yet finished with Sincerity's gift; I am netting her a reticule," she said.

"And what about me? What did you get for me?" he asked, smiling like a little boy.

"Oh, no you don't. Fool me once, shame on you; fool me twice, shame on me," laughed Chastity, both of them recalling the time when she was a little girl, and he had asked that question. She had blurted out what she had gotten for him, and then, realizing her blunder, she had burst into tears.

His brief laughter faded, and he grasped her hand tightly, saying, "Don't be too harsh on Alex. He is a fine young man."

Chastity's eyes sparkled with anger, a fire she had never before turned on her father. She stopped, her actions causing a ripple of missed steps among the other dancers in their set.

"I take exception to your definition of 'fine', Papa, if you will apply it to him." With this, she left the floor, her head held high. She found the ladies' withdrawing room and hid, still trembling with anger.

What was her father about? She had thought him infallible, perfect. But he was only a man, after all.

"Did you see her?" whispered Tranquility as she entered the room.

From behind her screen, Chastity heard her other sister giggle. "Only for a second. Then I spied Mama watching from her seat beside Lady Ravenwood. She turned puce with fury!"

"Big sister has done it now!" said Tranquility gleefully. "Imagine, leaving Papa standing on the dance floor!"

Chastity heard the door open and caught the end of

her mother's hearty, ". . . poor dear hasn't been feeling well all day. I tried to tell her to stay home, but she was so anxious to come."

"I do hope she's alright," gushed Lady Costain, before the door closed.

"Chastity!" said her mother sharply. "Tranquility, Sincerity, leave us!"

Chastity heard the key turn in the lock behind her sisters, and she came out to face her mother.

"What on earth possessed you?"

"Do not press me, Mother," said Chastity flatly.

Her mother paused, shaking her head. "Never did I think to witness such a spectacle." Chastity started to speak, but her mother waved her silent and began to pace. "I know how infuriating your father can be! But Chastity, to leave him standing on the dance floor! Only think of the scandal! No matter what he said . . . Why, even when he threw that *woman* in my face, I never would have dreamed of causing such a scene. That was why he did it there, of course, at Lady Sefton's ball." Lady Hartford sought the nearest chair, sinking down weakly before she continued, talking more to herself than to her daughter. "I didn't care about his going to her bed. I mean, that was a relief. The twins were only a year old, and I knew I never wanted . . . But to tell me about her! And in public!" She ceased her ramblings and focused on Chastity for the first time. "But I didn't leave him standing on the ballroom floor, Chastity! Only think of the scandal! And I can endure anything but scandal!"

Chastity closed her mouth, which had dropped open; her eyes filled with tears. She knelt by her mother and said quietly, "I'll go back out and tell everyone I tore the flounce on my gown."

Her mother grasped her hands and nodded vigorously. "Yes, yes, that's it! And you must dance! Dance every dance you can. And dance with your father again."

Chastity shook her head. "I can't, Mother."

"Can't? Of course you can! Didn't I?" Lady Hartford rose and squared her shoulders. Taking Chastity's arm, they left the sanctuary of the ladies' withdrawing room and entered the ballroom together.

Chastity smiled and danced and danced and danced. Young men, old men, she accepted every invitation, her jaw muscles aching with her forced smile.

Inside, however, she was grappling with the realization that her father was not the perfect man she had thought him. Not accustomed to feeling sympathy for her mother, she was overwhelmed. But she couldn't ignore the truth. She was no longer a child, she told herself ruthlessly as she danced and spoke of trivialities; she had to face the fact that her parents, neither of them, were perfect.

Her mother's revelations had been earth-shattering, coming fast, as they had, after her father's words about Alex. She could have excused her father's defense of Alex since he knew nothing of the affair with the comtesse. But to find her father had been lying, playing her mother false all these years!

Chastity had thought her father a beau ideal. Now, she found his tolerance of her mother was due to other interests, not to his divine patience. What else had he lied about? she wondered frantically. She took a deep breath and calmed herself. He was still her father, still the one person she had turned to all her life. She would have to accept that he was not an epic hero.

Alex watched from the edge of the dance floor, the scowl on his face deepening with each brilliant smile or tinkling laugh. He had started off telling himself it was all a show to make him jealous. But as her gaiety continued, and the line of gentlemen begging for a dance lengthened, he was not so sure. She was even dancing with Ravenwood and enjoying herself. And Ravenwood was gazing at her like a lovesick puppy.

It was the gown! Alex told himself—that emerald green gown that matched her eyes! When he had first seen her in the lamplight on the steps, he hadn't noticed how revealing it was, not at all her usual style. He couldn't like the cut of it, exposing, as it did, half her breasts! What was her mother about, allowing Chastity to wear such a gown!

The music ended, and Alex found himself pushing his way through the dancers, taking Chastity's arm before her other admirers could steal her away.

"I want to talk to you," he said gruffly, having no idea what he planned to talk about.

She disengaged his hand. "I don't wish to talk to you, Mr. Fitzsimmons," she said haughtily.

"Chastity!" he whispered fiercely, taking her arm again, and turning her around. The words of reproach he had planned were forgotten as he looked into her eyes, and he pleaded, "Please, Chastity, dance with me."

"I'm afraid the next dance is taken," she said.

"Chastity," he growled.

"And the next, and the next, and the next!"

Lord Petersham's smiling face appeared before her, and she took his arm blindly, leaving Alex behind. Trembling with emotion, Chastity began the dance, her steps automatic, her hopes dead.

"Mr. Fitzsimmons was a bit upset, I'm afraid," said Lord Petersham after watching her in silence for a few minutes.

"Hm," she grunted.

"I would have stepped aside if you'd told me," he said kindly, that fatuous smile of his awakening Chastity's attention.

"Certainly not, my lord. I have the partner I wanted,"

she added with a brilliant smile, causing his wide girth to swell larger still with pride.

"Thank you, my dear. Even we old men like to hear compliments. But I had the impression Alex was very anxious to talk to you."

"It was nothing, I'm sure." Her voice was lifeless.

"Oh, I see," he began doubtfully. But nothing affected the smiling Lord Petersham for very long, and he laughed. "I'm very pleased to be helping him out, you know. A very brave thing he's doing."

The steps of the dance separated them, and Chastity wanted to ignore the dictates of her mother and society, yank Lord Petersham aside, and demand an explanation. Instead, she waited impatiently to meet up with him again.

"What did you mean, Lord Petersham?" she asked quickly.

He gave an uncomfortable cough and mumbled, "Nothing at all, my dear. Nothing at all. Shouldn't have said anything. Security and all."

Chastity spent the rest of the set trying to pry more facts out of Lord Petersham, but she met with no success.

When the dance was over, Chastity looked for Alex, but he was nowhere in sight. Next, she sought out her father, who tried to ignore her. Insisting, Chastity dragged him away from his cronies and onto the dance floor, the only place they could safely talk.

"Tell me about Alex," she demanded immediately.

Her father looked down his aristocratic nose at her and sniffed. "Odd. You didn't wish to talk about him before."

Chastity expelled an exasperated sigh and tried again. "Please, Papa, tell me what Alex is up to."

"I don't know what you mean," he said, smiling as they were separated.

When they came back together, Chastity's expression was crafty. "What was your mistress's name?" she asked, watching him intently.

Her graceful father missed his step and trod on her foot. "Your mother should wash your mouth out with soap."

"I don't think so, since I had the truth from her lips. How could you, Papa? And breaking the news to her at Lady Sefton's ball!" she asked, losing her composure momentarily.

"So she told you about that. Did she tell you she'd just refused—again—to give me another child, possibly a son?"

The steps took them apart, and when they met again, Chastity was subdued.

"No, Papa, she neglected to tell me that."

"Besides, she didn't care then, and she doesn't care now—as long as I'm discreet. And I am very discreet."

"Papa! You have a mistress now?" gasped Chastity, reeling as if from a physical blow.

"Not *a* mistress. *The* mistress."

"The same woman? Why, she must be . . ."

"Forty years old. Yes, but she's one of my best friends." Chastity went limp on his arm, and he said anxiously, "I've shocked you. I'm sorry. You should never have been dragged into this sordid mess."

She shook her head. The music came to an end, and she leaned heavily on her father's arm as they left the dance floor. Her face had gone white, and when her father waved away her next partner, he left without comment.

"Papa, tell me the truth about Alex," she said softly.

"It's not my place. You'll have to ask him."

"But he's not here!"

"I know. When you refused to dance with him, he

came to tell me he was leaving. You'll have to wait until tomorrow."

"I'm so confused, so tired."

"Why don't you go home? My groom can drive you."

Chastity hesitated, looking around the elegant ballroom one more time. Then she nodded; there was nothing left for her there.

It was just past one o'clock in the morning when Chastity arrived home, met at the door by an anxious Petrie.

Removing her shawl, she asked, "What is it?"

"It's Cook, Miss Chastity!"

"Is she ill?" asked Chastity, pulling off her long kid gloves and heading toward the kitchens.

"No, no, she was staying with her daughter tonight because James told her he had extra chores to catch up on here."

"Yes?" said Chastity, wishing he would tell his tale faster.

"Jane is having the baby, so Cook came back to fetch James. Only James isn't here. Hale said he left this afternoon. Then Cook fainted dead away!"

"Where is she now?" asked Chastity, quickly glancing around the empty kitchen.

"She's gone back to her daughter. I sent Tim for the doctor."

"Good, then we don't have to worry about Jane or Cook. Only James."

"James is a no-account—"

"Not now, Petrie. There's not time for that. Have you seen Mr. Fitzsimmons?" she asked over her shoulder as she started toward the back stairs.

The butler was clearly puzzled by her question. "No,

miss, I haven't seen him come in. I thought he went to the Simpkins' ball with the family."

"So he did," said Chastity thoughtfully. "Tell Hale to have my horse saddled. Or if Baby is gone, tell him to saddle my father's gelding."

"But Miss Chastity, you can't mean to go out now!" Petrie exclaimed in horror.

"I mean exactly that, Petrie, and I refuse to stand here and have you question my orders. See to it immediately!"

Under such fierce determination, the butler crumbled and bowed to her will.

Chastity hurried up the stairs to her room, where she threw off her elegant ballgown and donned her old, navy habit. As she sat on the bed to tie her boots, her eyes fell on an envelope on the bedside table.

Recognizing the writing, she picked it up gingerly, frowning when something heavy inside it slid to one side. She opened it and pulled out a delicate gold chain. On the chain were a tiny skeleton key of gold filigree and a small gold heart.

Her breath coming faster, Chastity opened the single sheaf of note paper.

My dearest Chastity,

I hope you like your Christmas present. I had it made especially for my scavenger hunt partner, and I couldn't wait to give it to her. Please forgive me if I hurt you, but duty had to come first.

Once I finish this nasty business tonight, I'll come to your room and explain everything. I love you.

A

Chastity reread it twice, her first reactions of surprise and joy tempered by doubt and reason.

He loves me, she thought happily. But he says nothing about marriage, she reminded herself roughly. Perhaps he thought an offer of marriage unnecessary considering her reputation.

On this lowering thought, Chastity walked to the mirror and fastened the pendant around her neck. In the candlelight, the gold shimmered against the dark fabric of her habit. She touched the key, watching her image in the mirror.

What had the note said again? Chastity returned to the bed and picked up the paper. "I love you," he had written. Alex Fitzsimmons had written that he loved her. A feeling of wonder overcame her; her knees grew weak, and she sat down abruptly.

Suddenly, she didn't care about anything except that one sentence, that one fact—he loved her! And she loved him! And he hadn't been buying jewelry for the comtesse. It had been for her. So he wasn't having an affair with the comtesse.

"And he's not a spy or smuggler!" she said out loud, leaping up. If he were, she reasoned, he wouldn't be writing about "nasty business." He was on the right side, their side, and her father, (God bless him), knew it, but hadn't been at liberty to explain it all. And neither had Alex!

In an instant, everything had been made crystal clear. The comtesse, being French, was a suspect in his investigation. The nightly rides to the beach, to the comtesse's house, all had been undertaken as part of his duty. Even the attempt on his life . . .

Chastity turned white with fright, grabbed her riding gloves, and headed for the door. In the front hall, she had to fight her way past Petrie and Hale, who had joined forces and insisted she take an armed escort. But she forestalled them both, saying, "James will be there; I'll come to no harm. And Mr. Fitzsimmons will be there, too. You are to tell no one I've gone. Do you understand?"

They agreed reluctantly. Chastity hurried into her father's study, shutting the door so her loyal servants would not be overset by the sight of their young mistress loading two miniature single-shot pistols. She slipped one into each pocket of her habit and retraced her steps. Promising over and over again to be careful, she mounted her father's gelding and rode off.

Alex felt better than he had all evening as he rode toward the smugglers' cove. He had left the note for Chastity and was relieved the lies were over and done with. She might reject him and his love, but he had been honest, and now he could concentrate on the task at hand.

He patted the stallion's glossy neck, thankful there was no moon to show his presence. He dismounted and left Baby tethered just inside the trees.

Crouching low, he made his way to the edge of the cliff not far from where the path led down to the beach. Lying on the ground, he pulled out his spyglass and trained it on the Channel. The sliver of a moon gave nothing away, so he turned it on the beach.

Here, he was luckier. Pulled up to the old dock was a boat. Though they did their work in near darkness, an occasional lantern was unshuttered, and Alex was able to count their numbers. There were perhaps four or five who remained on the boat. On shore, unloading and loading boxes, there appeared to be seven men.

The one giving orders was tall and extremely slender, his dark hair pulled back and tied in a queue. So that was why the "comtesse" had not made an appearance at the Simpkins' ball.

Alex froze, listening to the struggles of someone

climbing up the steep path. Then there was another noise beside him. The hair on the back of his neck standing on end, he turned suddenly, looking straight up. Expecting to find the enemy, he tensed for battle.

"Alex," whispered Chastity before she was knocked to the ground. Alex half-covered her body with his, his large hand turning her face so that it was sheltered against his chest.

"Shh," was all he would say.

Chastity ceased her struggles as she, too, heard the man reach the top of the path. Alex stiffened as a lantern was opened in signal; then the man closed it and moved farther along the cliffs, whistling out of key.

Alex whispered against her ear, "I should spank you." She shook her head imperceptibly. Alex grinned to himself and began kissing her ear, his tongue outlining each delicate curve until Chastity shuddered, sighing loudly.

She turned her head to meet his lips and all was forgotten as she received his kiss. It was light and brief, causing Chastity to wriggle with impatience. Smiling, Alex obliged her with another, this time a tender, lingering kiss.

Then he moved his head, speaking softly into her ear. "That will have to do, my love, until I am finished with this business. But afterward," here he paused and kissed her ear before continuing, "when we are married, I promise I shan't stop at that."

"Married?" she said, her voice slicing through the stillness like a knife.

Alex didn't wait to see where the guard was, he leapt to his feet and met the assault with a head butt to the man's stomach.

"Run!" he yelled at Chastity, who had also risen and was trying to help Alex, her efforts only getting in his way.

Shouts from below rent the air.

"Get out of here!" he yelled again, pushing her toward the trees before punching his opponent in the eye, sending the man reeling. "Go on!"

"No! Not without you!" Chastity screamed back.

The smuggler lunged forward. Alex sidestepped him, landing a blow to the man's kidneys.

With a fierceness she had never thought to possess, Chastity balled up her hand and struck the man's jaw as he fell.

"Come on!" yelled Alex, an absurd grin on his face.

Chastity stretched out her hand to him, but he was hauled backward by a new opponent. Chastity looked past Alex and saw another head appear at the cliff's edge.

With a savage assault, Alex downed his man and started toward her, and Chastity ran, never looking back until she reached the trees. Spinning around to locate Alex, she screamed his name.

He was still on his feet fighting, but another man had made it up the steep hill. And then there were two more.

"For God's sake, get out of here!"

Still, she hesitated, heartsick with fear for him. Chastity felt the small pistols in her pockets. They would only make the spies laugh, and there were not enough charges to take care of all of them.

She whirled around, ran into the wood, untied her father's gelding, and hit his flank as hard as she could. The horse whinnied and took off in the direction of the barn. Chastity hitched up her skirts and climbed the nearest tree. Wiping tears from her eyes, she surveyed the battleground.

"There's another one—a girl!" said the first spy to his cohorts as he wiped blood from his face. He kicked Alex's still body. "Bloody exciseman!"

"Never mind him for now," said a familiar voice, and Chastity strained to catch what was said. "See if you can find the girl." Two men headed toward the trees and Chastity's perch. She held tight, not daring to breathe.

"If they don't find her?" said another voice with a heavy French accent.

"It doesn't matter. We'll be away long before she can cause trouble," said the other Frenchman.

"What about him? Shall I kill him?" asked the first eagerly.

"No, not yet, we may have need of a hostage."

Chastity breathed a sigh of relief. She listened carefully, trying to place the familiar voice. Then it hit her—the comtesse! But it was a man speaking! With dawning awareness, she realized that the comtesse, the woman all the men had swarmed around, was, in reality, a man. She smiled despite the gravity of her situation.

Had Alex known? she wondered. But of course he had. That was why he had laughed so when she had accused him of buying jewels for the comtesse. That, and the fact that he loved her, of course. Chastity gasped for breath as a sob rose in her throat.

One of the men passed beneath her hide-out. "Find anything, James?"

Chastity forced herself to remain motionless, letting the tears stream silently down her cheeks.

"Nothing, Henry," said James softly. "I don't like this. My Jane will be worried sick. Let's finish loading and get out of here."

"I'm with you."

They returned to the comtesse and the other men, one of whom Chastity now recognized as the gatekeeper. She watched as they dragged Alex to the edge of the cliff. The gatekeeper lifted Alex's body over one shoulder and started down, the others following quickly. Only the one guard was left on the cliffs.

Chastity settled herself on her perch. She would have to wait for help, if it came. Surely it would if her father's horse made it all the way back to the barn riderless. Of course, there was a deal of grass on the way, and the gelding might simply stop to graze.

If help didn't come, it would be up to her. She fingered the small guns again. She would wait until the guard started down the cliff; then she would follow. Surely James would help her if a confrontation arose. Or perhaps the smugglers would simply leave Alex behind. Alive, she prayed. She would not contemplate any other possibility.

Alex frowned, not daring to open his eyes; the pain in his head was so fierce that he was glad to be lying down. He tried to shift his position, but found his hands and feet bound. Cautiously, he opened his eyes and took note of his surroundings. He was on the beach, lying on his side with something firm behind him, presumably a box. In front of him, men moved quickly and silently. He turned his head; judging from the position of the moon, he had only been unconscious a short time.

"Almost finished, St. Pierre," said the dwarf-like Jean-Jacques.

"Good," replied the "Comtesse de St. Pierre."

"What shall we do with him?" asked Jean-Jacques, jerking his head in Alex's direction.

"When we get out in the Channel, we'll throw him overboard. Until then, we'll keep him alive."

The servant grunted, satisfied but impatient.

Alex began to work at the ropes binding his wrists. He looked around the beach; at least, he thought, Chastity had not been captured. Perhaps she would come with help, perhaps not. He didn't know where she could get help. Most of the locals wouldn't dare interfere with smugglers, and Lieutenant Humphries and his men would be waiting for his signal, a signal he was unable to send.

This was not a good situation, he told himself dryly. If he hadn't been playing around with Chastity instead of paying attention to his job, he might be heading toward a soft bed by now. But self-recrimination was not Alex's style, and he continued working on the ropes, his mind grappling with plans for extrication from his very bleak predicament.

Suddenly Alex found himself hauled to his feet, and he groaned at the pain this awoke. Ignoring this, he looked down into St. Pierre's face and smiled.

"At least you chose to keep your real name. I didn't think you would want me to call you comtesse anymore," he said affably.

St. Pierre sneered at him and said derisively, "Why do I care what you foolish Englishmen call me?" He preened and said, "You were surprised to find you had been lusting after a man, eh?"

Alex laughed, his words causing the Frenchman to glower at him. "I hate to disappoint you," he began, stressing "disappoint." "But I saw through your disguise long ago. You make a very poor woman; of course, you're almost as bad a man." Alex reeled as a blow caught his chin. Jean-Jacques kept him on his feet, and Alex was able to face his enemy with another infuriating smile.

He braced himself for the next impact, but St. Pierre only grunted and said, "I should have killed you that day after you left the inn with Miss Hartford."

"Can't seem to get anything right, eh?" taunted Alex.

St. Pierre stiffened, but ignored the insult. He called to his men, *"Vite! Vite!* We set sail in a few minutes!" Then he turned to Alex and said, "You will be going with us, Mr. Fitzsimmons, but only for a short ride."

"Step away from him," said Chastity, her voice and hands quivering as she held her two weapons on St. Pierre. From behind Alex, Jean-Jacques laughed. Chastity never took her eyes from St. Pierre. "If you do not untie Mr. Fitzsimmons, I will gladly shoot your master. You will notice that both guns are cocked and ready to fire."

"And they are such fierce guns," said the rumpled servant with another mirthless laugh.

"Shut your mouth, you fool. They are big enough! Do as she bids," said St. Pierre.

Grumbling, Jean-Jacques cut Alex's bonds.

"The knife, old man," said Alex, holding out his hand.

The servant stretched out his hand with the knife in his palm. In a flash, the knife was slicing into Alex's hand, and he leapt away. St. Pierre grabbed Chastity's hands, and they struggled for control. The gun went off and one of the French sailors fell. Alex ran into the cave, knocking down surprised smugglers as he went. Remi, the gatekeeper, started after him, but fell mysteriously as he passed James.

During the argument which ensued on the beach, Alex managed to escape, never faltering as he passed from the cave into the passageway that led to the comtesse's house. He entered the ground floor and hurried outdoors, retracing his steps, this time above ground. He thought his lungs would burst, but he knew he had to make it to the bonfire, the signal he had set for Lieutenant Humphries. It was the only way he could save Chastity.

If he was not too late, warned a pessimistic voice within.

Chapter Eight

St. Pierre ordered everyone on board, pulling out a very deadly-looking pistol when several of the locals balked. They had agreed to unload the boat, not to sail off to France, they said. The regulars laughed at them, taunting them for their cowardice, and St. Pierre promised them death if they didn't do as ordered.

Chastity was bound and gagged and thrown on board. In vain did she look for Alex; he never reappeared. She knew he had a job to do, but she had assumed he would rescue her. She tried to comfort herself with thoughts of Alex planning her rescue, but it was difficult as the boat was pushed off, and they set sail.

"So he does not come back to save you," said St. Pierre, kneeling down and caressing her hair until she pulled away in disgust. "Why do you care for him? These Englishmen are so cold and distant. They have no passion; perhaps you should try a Frenchman." He laughed and went to stand at the side, scanning the horizon for signs of trouble.

James and Henry watched also, their faces troubled.

"This is more than I bargained for, Henry," James whispered. "Miss Chastity deserves better from me. And from you, too. Didn't she help yer mother out after yer father was killed?"

"Yeah, she was there all th' time. But what can we do? We can't back out now," said Henry. "I should have listened to you," he added forlornly.

"Aye, and I shouldn't have listened to you. But now we're here; we've got to do something. We'll just keep our eyes peeled for the main chance, right?"

Henry nodded and strolled away. James moved closer to St. Pierre and Jean-Jacques, seemingly intent on inspecting the rigging.

"I do not like it that Fitzsimmons got away," Jean-Jacques was saying. "He will go straight to the militia."

St. Pierre laughed. "And what will they do? Walk on water? I told you their boat is in dry dock for repairs. They can't come after us."

"I'm not so sure."

St. Pierre clapped him on the back and said, "You and your worries! You are an old woman, Jean-Jacques! They'll never . . ." He gripped the rail, his eyes glued to the disappearing shoreline. On the distant cliffs, a flame had appeared, growing larger and larger as they watched.

"Mon Dieu!" whispered Remi who had joined them. "Look! There's another one!"

And in the distance, toward Folkestone, they could see another bonfire spring to life.

"And another!" exclaimed Jean-Jacques. "Do you still think I am an old woman, St. Pierre? Why would they be signaling if they didn't have a way to come after us? You are the fool!"

"Captain!" bellowed St. Pierre, turning to the red-faced captain. "Don't you see the signals? Can't this boat go any faster?"

The argument that followed was loud and accompanied by many gestures. James knelt behind Chastity and began sawing at the ropes that bound her wrists. "Miss Chastity, we're going over th' side. We're taking a dinghy. You stay close; Henry and me, we'll look after you."

She nodded and crawled after him toward the back of the boat. Henry and James, along with Sam, another local, were just untying the small boat when the alarm was sounded.

"Stop them!" yelled Remi.

"Get them!" echoed Jean-Jacques, wading into the melee without hesitation. In the struggle, Chastity was knocked to the deck, her ankle stepped on, her body battered. She made her way to the dinghy to untie it, but long, bony fingers closed painfully over her hands, and she cried out.

St. Pierre hauled her to her feet and threw her toward Remi. "Tie her up," he ordered.

"Now can we kill them all?" asked Jean-Jacques triumphantly. With a satisfied grunt, he kicked James's inert form.

"Throw the men over. We'll keep the girl. They won't dare attack with her on board."

Chastity screamed, "No!" as they tossed the unconscious James overboard. Henry and Sam begged to be spared, but their pleas were ignored.

As Henry was climbing over the rail at gunpoint, he said desperately, "I can't swim!"

This brought on a spate of laughter from Remi and Jean-Jacques.

"Afraid you might drown?" asked Remi cruelly.

"Count your blessings, *mon ami*. You will die more quickly that way!" added Jean-Jacques, giving Henry a final thrust.

Chastity put her hands over her ears and pressed hard to shut out Henry's last screams.

"So much for your gallant friends," sneered St. Pierre, hauling her to her feet and forcing her to the railing. "You mustn't be impolite, Miss Hartford. Bid them good-bye."

With that, Chastity swooned for the first time in her life.

Alex mounted Chastity's stallion and turned him toward Folkestone. The pounding of the hoofs beat out a tattoo of desperation, and he kept the big horse at a gallop. He finally pulled up when he reached the second bonfire, throwing the reins to the waiting militia man.

"Rub him down and let him rest. Then take him back to Hartford House, will you?"

"Yes, sir," said the young man with a snappy salute.

"Have you seen them yet?"

"No, sir. The third fire went off ten minutes ago, so they should be here soon."

With a grunt, Alex began lowering himself down the side of the cliff. The water below had proven deep enough for Lord Petersham's yacht, and they were to pick him up there. The only obstacle had been how to arrive at the base of the cliffs without killing himself. There was no pathway, so two lengths of stout rope had been joined—joined well, Alex hoped, as he slid down the side toward the deep water. There wasn't a beach below, just a narrow ledge and then the Channel.

He heard the boat before he saw it. Then it appeared around the bend, lights blazing. He could see the crew and militiamen busy on deck. As it drew closer, a dinghy was lowered.

Alex was greeted by Lieutenant Humphries with a quick salute followed by an enthusiastic grin.

"Smashing night for a spy hunt, sir."

"Yes, but there's been a twist added. Miss Hartford is, in all likelihood, on board their boat."

"Miss Hartford! Don't tell me she's part . . ." began

the lieutenant. Alex raised one withering brow, and the young officer blushed. "No, no, of course not. But how?"

"She was playing knight-errant. There was a confrontation—two of them, actually. She was trying to rescue me, not knowing about our plan to capture them at sea. They had been planning to take me along as a hostage. Now, I assume, they will have taken her instead."

"How did you get away?"

"Never mind that. We've got to make sure everyone knows she's there so she won't get hurt. There will be no question now of using Lord Petersham's toy."

"Without the cannon, I don't see how we can hope to stop them, sir."

"We may not be able to board them. We may have to run them to ground," Alex said with relish. He smiled as the lieutenant blanched, his eyes like saucers in the lantern light. "Never been in hand-to-hand combat with the French before, Lieutenant?"

"No, sir, nor with anyone else."

"It's not so different from maneuvers, except they'll have real guns and knives to fight back. Besides," Alex added more seriously, "there are several Englishmen who were forced to go along."

"Aye, smugglers."

"No, good men who saw a chance to earn a little ready the easy way this one time. When it comes to a fight, they'll be our allies; I'd stake my life on it," said Alex.

"That's exactly what we'll be doing, Captain."

"Lieutenant! There's something in the water up ahead!"

Alex and Humphries hurried to the bow and peered into the darkness below. They lowered a grappling hook; as they raised it, one man leaned over with a lantern.

"*Ahh!*" he yelled, jumping back. "It's a body!"

They pulled the dead man on board and turned him over. "Local man. Can't place his name," said the lieutenant.

"Hey! Hallo the boat! Hey!"

The men flew back to the rail and peered into the darkness.

"Hey! Over here!"

When the two men had been brought on board, Alex asked anxiously, "Where's Chastity? James!"

James accepted a hot cup of tea and whiskey and cupped it in his hands, shaking his head dolefully. "She's still on board, Mr. Fitzsimmons. Henry and me and Sam, we tried to rescue her, but they caught us. Sam, there, couldn't swim, and he drowned right quick. I was unconscious when I hit the water, but the cold brought me around. Henry and I have been treading water and swimming ever since."

"I told them I couldn't swim—thought maybe they'd show a little mercy," said Henry with a bitter laugh. "They just laughed and shoved me in. Poor Sam, 'e really didn't know how to swim, and 'e panicked. We couldn't hold 'im afloat."

"How far ahead would you say they are?" asked Alex.

"Twenty minutes, I'd say."

Alex nodded. "Lieutenant, tell the captain to raise the sail and give it all the steam he's got. Looks like we're going to France."

Chastity closed her eyes, unable to stay awake another minute. She would need to be rested, she reasoned, when she got wherever it was she was going. She knew Alex would come for her; it was just a question of when. With this, she fell asleep, her dreams full of hope and sweet kisses.

When Chastity opened her eyes, she noticed the sky had lightened to a dull gray; it had grown colder and there were dark clouds above. She struggled to sit up and stretched furtively, not wanting to call attention to herself. She looked over the side of the boat.

Ahead, she saw the white cliffs of France. Odd, she thought; it looked almost like home. They were approaching the coastline, but there was no town, no buildings—only countryside.

A cry went up from the crew, and Chastity turned around. On the horizon, she could just make out the shape of a ship.

"Come here," growled Jean-Jacques, dragging her roughly to her feet and propelling her toward the rear of the boat. "We're going to put you up here where your friends will be able to see you." Chastity struggled, but it was hopeless; she was lashed to a large crate, facing the distant ship.

Was it Alex? But of course it was! she told herself firmly. No one else would be sailing from England to France. They had probably been closing in all night. How, she didn't know, since she, too, had thought Lieutenant Humphries was without a ship.

St. Pierre appeared beside her, a spyglass to his eye as he surveyed the distant ship. He held the apparatus up to her eye and asked, "What ship is that? Do you know it?"

Chastity smiled at him and said saucily, "Yes, I know it, and you'll never outrun it. It's a steam-powered boat. Much too fast for this thing."

Chastity braced herself for his anger, but he only laughed. "But you forget, my dear, we have almost reached France, and there, I have the advantage."

"You think this motley crew can defeat good English militia men? You know those bonfires were the signal to the militia, and you know they're on board."

He smiled and curled his bony fingers around her chin, forcing her head back so she had to look him in the eye. "You are so innocent. I will leave Remi here to face the brave and gallant soldiers while Jean-Jacques and I go ashore. You too, *'certainement.'* "

"Me? But why not leave me here? Then Alex will leave you alone."

He released her chin roughly. "What you propose is so very tempting," he said, his hand slipping down her side and coming to rest at her waist. Chastity shut her eyes tight. Then he removed his hand and said briskly, "But you are wrong, Miss Hartford. I know many men like your Mr. Fitzsimmons. He would see you safe, then he would come after me. It is a matter of duty with these fools. He was told, no doubt, to either capture me, or kill me. No, I have no choice; he will force me to meet him, and I would rather it be on my terms, on my territory."

"Where are you taking me?" she asked with a toss of her head.

"I have been given, awarded, if you will, a small château. It is very old and boasts a moat and a drawbridge. That is the only entrance. I will meet him there. And I will kill him," he said, a grim smile forming on his lips.

Chastity shivered.

Alex lowered the glass and handed it to the lieutenant, his face rigid with hate. "She's still alive, at least. He's got her tied up there for us to see."

"A warning," commented the lieutenant, lowering the glass in turn.

"Yes. I wish I knew what he was planning," said Alex, looking at the boat ahead, at Chastity. He hoped she was not too frightened. He grinned; knowing her temper, it was probably St. Pierre who was uneasy.

"Maybe we can negotiate with him. We'll leave him alone if he gives us the girl," suggested Humphries.

"If I thought he could be trusted, I'd do it. But he can't. And anyway, I want him: alive, if possible; dead, if not. Either way, he's mine. Watch her," he commanded. "I'm going to get ready."

Alex went below where the ship's cook had set an elegant table for the crew and soldiers—Lord Petersham's idea of a proper breakfast, no doubt. He sat down and was offered an assortment of muffins, coddled eggs, kidney pie, and black coffee. He accepted the coffee and a muffin.

When he had finished this, Alex went to the arsenal the lieutenant had provided and selected two pistols and a deadly-looking knife. He loaded the pistols and took extra ammunition. Then he picked out a musket, sighting it on the door to the galley and frightening the ship's cabin boy, who came in carrying another tray of food.

Alex went back on board; they were drawing closer. Chastity was still in sight, he noted with relief. He hoped St. Pierre would leave her and run, but he doubted it. St. Pierre was not so foolish; he knew Chastity provided him with a certain degree of safety. The Frenchman wouldn't readily give that up.

"Load the cannon, Lieutenant," Alex said softly.

"Captain?" said Humphries, unable to hide his surprise. Alex nodded, and the young officer protested, "But Miss Hartford! You can't mean to use the cannon with her on board!"

"To be quite honest, Humphries, I don't think she'll be on board for very long after they reach the shore. Look ahead there, at that carriage. You mark my words; St. Pierre will run, and he'll take Chastity with him!"

"Surely he won't leave his men defenseless!" exclaimed Humphries, his sense of duty and fair play outraged.

Alex shrugged. "He'll leave them. And when he does, when I give the signal, fire the cannon. Aim below the waterline. It should sink fast, but the crew will be fine until you can pick them up."

"Some may escape."

"True, but it's St. Pierre we really want. I'd like his employer, too, but I daresay we shan't be that lucky. If it's who I think it is, he's too wily to be caught. The main thing is to keep St. Pierre from setting up the same operation somewhere else along our coastline."

"Yes, sir," said Humphries, turning to order the loading of the six-pound cannon.

Chastity hit her head as the boat touched the shore. Then Jean-Jacques cut the rope binding her to the crate and dragged her toward the front of the boat, and France. She struggled against him, but he was surprisingly strong for his size, and she found herself being thrown from the vessel to the ground.

Standing up again, she was thrust into a dilapidated carriage. Jean-Jacques climbed onto the box and St. Pierre got inside, ignoring her as he shouted his final instructions to Remi.

"And Remi, if you get the chance, kill Fitzsimmons!"

"No!" screamed Chastity, kicking St. Pierre soundly and trying to throw herself out of the carriage.

Inexorably, she was pulled back and slapped across the face for her efforts.

"Be quiet, wench, or I'll make you wish you had!"

Chastity fell back, subdued, into the corner of the vehicle. She could feel a trickle of blood running down her chin from the corner of her mouth, but with her hands ied, she could do nothing about it. She ran her tongue across her swollen lip.

For the first time, she was frightened. She was on foreign soil, in a hostile country. Alex, if he escaped being killed by the other spies, might not be able to find her. She shivered, wanting to cry, but not wanting to show any weakness before the Frenchman.

Then she heard the sound of muskets popping, some close, some distant, as Lord Petersham's yacht came into range. She peered out the window, and was able to see both vessels. Suddenly there was a boom and a burst of smoke from the yacht. Then the carriage turned away from the shore, and she lost sight of both boats, and of Alex.

Chastity closed her eyes, pretending to sleep so that St. Pierre wouldn't bother her. She peeked through her lashes at him occasionally, studying him. He had a gun in his coat pocket, she knew. There was another tucked into his pants. There was no way of knowing if the guns were loaded, but she imagined they must be. He seemed a very thorough man.

Jean-Jacques posed another problem. When they arrived at this château, would there be other servants? St. Pierre having called his residence a château, she assumed it would be staffed. However, since St. Pierre had been living in England for the past six months, perhaps he had dismissed the others. Remi and Jean-Jacques were possibly his only servants from the château. If so, perhaps she would have a chance.

Chastity pretended to awake and stared out the window, taking in every turn they made. The sun was in front of them, so they were heading due east, parallel with the coastline. If she escaped, she would have to try and retrace her way to the landing if she hoped to meet up with Alex. If he was still alive.

Chastity forced away this negative thought. They

traveled on for another hour before turning off the road, and inland. Looking out at the sun, she judged it to be around nine o'clock.

Half an hour later, they turned into a run-down gate. A few outbuildings, all in disrepair, came into view. And finally, the château. It was small and situated on top of a hill with no trees around, making it impossible to launch a successful surprise attack. The house was enclosed in a compound and did have a moat, though there was little water in it. The building itself was in poor condition and looked deserted.

"You seem to have a fondness for derelict properties," Chastity taunted, sitting up and yawning. St. Pierre only glared at her. She hoped her composure would unsettle him.

She watched their progress with interest. They crossed the drawbridge, which was already lowered. Then the carriage halted, and Jean-Jacques jumped to the ground, using a key to open a door beside the iron gate. Chastity heard the creaking of metal as the dwarf turned the wheel and raised the gate.

Panting, he climbed back on the box and drove through. St. Pierre opened the carriage door and pulled Chastity out into a neglected courtyard. She staggered, unable to get her balance with her hands tied. St. Pierre righted her, keeping one hand at her back. Jean-Jacques, she noticed, was leading the team off to the stable. There were no chickens scratching in the yard, no sign of life. And best of all, no other servants to be seen. She looked at the open gate hopefully.

From the house, the sound of a door opening made her heart sink. So there were others here after all. But the man approaching was anything but a servant. He was not very tall, but he presented an imposing figure in his elegant suit and many-caped coat. He bowed to her.

"St. Pierre, you should not mix business with pleasure," he said, nodding toward Chastity.

"Hardly pleasure, sir. She is my prisoner, and I am expecting a visit shortly from her lover, an Englishman, a spy."

"So? How will he find you? Have you grown so neglectful this past six months?"

St. Pierre was clearly discomfited by this comment and hastened to say, "No, sir. The contretemps was unavoidable. My identity had been guessed, and we were forced to leave suddenly. We will, of course, return to England when and where you say, sir."

Chastity watched with growing interest. The stranger, though he didn't look dangerous, was clearly a man of power, a man St. Pierre feared greatly.

"Alex will kill you first," she said to St. Pierre, watching the other man.

"Shut your mouth, wench," said St. Pierre.

"You speak French very well," said the stranger.

"Thank you, Mr . . . ?"

He smiled, but didn't satisfy her curiosity. He was a handsome man, but his smile made her uneasy; it showed a streak of cruelty.

"Do what you must, St. Pierre. I will be in contact with you later."

"Monsieur Talley . . ."

"No names," growled the stranger.

"Of course not. Sorry, sir," said St. Pierre anxiously.

"Good-bye, mademoiselle. So unfortunate that we shan't be able to meet again under better circumstances."

With an elegant bow, the stranger was gone, walking out the front gate. Seconds later, they heard the hoofbeats of a horse as it cantered away.

St. Pierre wiped the sweat from his brow, grunted, and said, "Don't worry, my dear Miss Hartford. We'll be safe enough until Jean-Jacques can lower the gate. In the meantime, let me show you my home."

Bowing gallantly, he pulled her across the courtyard into the house. The foyer was barren of furniture. In the salon, there were a few hard chairs, but nothing of comfort.

"Please, monsieur, I have need of a bit of privacy," she said, squirming convincingly.

He grunted and looked her over, considering. "Come in here," he said, leading her to a back room that had only one door. In it were a cot, a small dresser, and a chamber pot.

Chastity turned slightly and offered her hands. "Please," she asked docilely. St. Pierre looked around the room before untying her.

Chastity waited until he had closed the door. Then she quickly took care of business before prowling around the room and dresser looking for a weapon. There was nothing, and she scowled. Then she saw the bowl and pitcher on the dresser. Too large a weapon to surprise him, but it could prove very effective. And besides, she thought, what other choice did she have?

Chastity opened the drawers to the dresser noisily, hoping she could attract St. Pierre. He must have been standing just outside the door, for it flew open, and he crossed the tiny room in a blink of an eye. Chastity whirled around, grabbing the pitcher as she did, catching him flush in the face. It broke, and he stumbled backward, blood streaming down his face, blinding him. Chastity picked up the bowl and brought it down full force on his head. He fell to the floor, unconscious.

She rushed to the doorway, half-expecting to find Jean-Jacques. But he was still outside, she supposed, and she turned and took both pistols from St. Pierre.

Outside, Chastity moved cautiously. Hearing the creaking of the gate again, she looked over and found

Jean-Jacques staring at her, his mouth twisted into a sneer.

Chastity raised the pistol and screamed, "Get out of the way!"

The dwarf hesitated and Chastity crossed the courtyard, knowing her aim was not good. As she approached, he moved back from the gate, raising his hand. The look on his face was crafty, and Chastity had to fight down her sense of panic.

"Move over there," she ordered, pointing the gun toward the barn. Now what? she wondered desperately. She couldn't get away without a horse, but the horses were in the barn. She would have to force the little man to get one of the horses.

Chastity took a deep breath and said, "Come on. We're going to the barn."

With an unnerving smile, the little man turned, walking in front of her. Things were close in the barn, and Chastity held back, not wanting to get within arm's length of Jean-Jacques.

"Put a bridle on him," she said, motioning to one of the horses. Jean-Jacques did as he was bid. "Now bring both of them outside." Chastity stepped back into the yard, well away from the door.

"Leave the horses and get back in the barn," she said, waving the gun menacingly when he didn't comply.

"You will never get away, mademoiselle. You are simply making things worse for yourself. You will be taken to Paris, where *la guillotine* will separate you from your foolishness."

Chastity smiled at him and shook her head. She was in control now; his words told her so. Jean-Jacques backed into the barn. Chastity took a pitchfork and jammed it against the door. It wouldn't hold him long, but she only needed enough time to mount. She grabbed the halter of the extra horse and pulled him to the gate, slapping his flank to send him down the hillside. Then she went back to get the bridled horse. She looked around for a way to mount.

The steps of the house were the only possibility. She turned the pistol on the barn, guessing Jean-Jacques was watching as he tried to break out. Then she led the horse to the steps and gathered the reins and mane in one hand.

She swung her right leg up over the horse's back as she heard the door to the house bang open. Then she felt herself dragged down. She kicked furiously, but she couldn't get away, and the horse sidled away. Screaming, kicking, and hitting, she went to the ground.

Looking up, Chastity saw the enraged face of St. Pierre before his fist came crashing down on her. Then all went black.

Chapter Nine

Lord Petersham's yacht proved too large to get close into the shore, so they launched both dinghies as soon as they had fired the cannon. The confusion on board the smugglers' boat and on shore provided cover for their approach. Alex was on the first dinghy that landed, and they were met by a volley of musket shots followed by a disorderly charge. Lieutenant Humphries fired his musket once and then leapt ashore, fixing his bayonet and leading his men forward.

Alex did the same, but his eyes and thoughts were on the faint trail down which the carriage had disappeared. He was forcibly brought back to the present by Remi.

"Fitzsimmons!" bellowed the Frenchman, firing his pistol and missing. With a savage cry, he charged, knocking Alex to the ground.

Alex reached for his own pistol, but Remi kicked it from his grasp. Alex stumbled to his feet to meet the next assault. Remi growled and pulled out a knife.

"Now we will finish the job," he said.

Alex smiled and produced his own knife, saying, "One of us will, anyway."

They circled, lunging and retreating, ducking and swaying. Oblivious of the fighting going on around them, each man concentrated fiercely on his opponent.

Remi was taller and might have had the advantage, but for his age. The ten years or so between he and the younger man began to tell, and his strikes became ponderous and heavy-handed. He pinked Alex's arm and then reeled backward to avoid the retaliation. But he was tiring, and he fell, waving his knife as he clambered to his feet again.

"Give up, old man," said Alex, taunting him.

"Merde!" yelled Remi in frustration. He charged blindly, and Alex stepped to one side like a matador, and caught the Frenchman in the abdomen, plunging the knife in to the hilt.

Remi twisted and fell face up, and Alex bent over him.

"Where has he taken her? Tell me!"

Remi smiled, blood running from the corners of his mouth. Then he clutched Alex's arm and died.

Alex cursed, looking up sharply as a shadow fell across Remi's body.

"Looks like we've taken the fight out of them, sir," said Lieutenant Humphries with a grin. He had a tear in his red jacket, but other than that, he appeared none the worse for wear.

"How many of us do you want to go with you?" asked the young officer, his mood almost jocular.

Alex straightened up and surveyed the damage. One red-coated figure lay still on the ground. Another nursed his wounds but seemed to be alright. The smugglers huddled together. There were only four of them; two others were dead, and the rest had gotten away.

"None. I'll go alone."

"I must protest, sir. Two against one, at the very least. You don't know what you'll have to contend with. Let me go with you."

Alex shook his head. "No, I speak the language. I'll get along alright. The last thing I need is a red-coated

Englishman traveling across the French countryside with me. No, you go back to the boat with the prisoners. Sail out into the Channel and come back tonight. Hopefully, Miss Hartford and I will be here waiting."

"And if you're not?"

"Then come back the next night and the next. Give us three nights. If we're not back by then, sail back to England and give your report to the Home Office in London." At the mention of headquarters, Humphries came to attention. Alex smiled, then grew sober again as he continued, "You'll also be responsible for going to the Hartford's and informing them . . . Well, you know. But give me three nights first."

The lieutenant agreed reluctantly. He ordered the quartering of the prisoners and the burial of Remi and the other French smuggler. The young English soldier, they took on board to return his body home. Alex gathered his weapons together and accepted a bundle of food from the ship's cook.

He replied to Humphries's salute and then extended his hand. The lieutenant shook it in silence.

"Three nights," said Alex.

"I'll be here. Good luck, sir."

Alex turned and began walking down the path that led along the coastline. He didn't see a soul, not a farmhouse or even a cow. He walked for hours, seeing nothing but an occasional bird.

When he came to the fork in the road, he stooped down to study the ground. It was difficult to tell if the carriage had turned or not; the ruts were deep and hard going in both directions.

There was a crack of thunder, and he looked up. He could see the sheets of rain coming his way. It was a typical storm for the coast, loud and furious—and brief, he hoped. Alex pulled his hat down to keep the rain from seeping down his neck. With head down, he turned off on the side road, unable to look up because of the wind and rain coming straight at him.

Judging from the light, and this was difficult because the storm continued to dump rain relentlessly, Alex thought it was about four o'clock. He had an hour of light left before darkness settled in. Cold, wet, and disheartened, he continued doggedly on.

The wind had abated, but the rain was steady, drenching. Alex took refuge beneath a tree and pulled out the bread and cheese wrapped in oilcloth that the cook had given him. It was the first time he had eaten since that morning. He washed it down with rainwater caught in a tin cup.

From his soggy shelter, he surveyed the hillside, and that was when he saw it. He stood up, forgetting the food and cup. He took a step forward, then stopped. There was still too much light. Another hour would make it dark enough for his approach to be undetected. He settled back down on the ground and put his cup out in the rain to catch some more water. He finished the cheese and leaned back against the tree.

He was not afraid of falling asleep, despite the fact that he had not slept all night. His mind was filled with thoughts of Chastity, fear for her safety. But he fought down his sense of fear and desperation, concentrating instead on his memories of Chastity—the way she had looked at the Christmas balls, the sound of her laughter when they had ridden away with the coachman's whip, the feel of her lips on his.

When Chastity awoke, she thought she would faint again from the pain. She found that if she didn't move, the agony was almost bearable. So she lay where she was, in the dark, trying not to think about anything.

The door opened and the flood of light made her blink painfully.

"So, you are awake, you vixen," said Jean-Jacques. "Too bad. I had hoped St. Pierre had killed you."

Chastity couldn't answer him, so she remained still. The dwarf advanced into the tiny room and stood over the bed.

"You are more trouble than you are worth, I told him. But I think he has other plans for you." With this the little man gave an evil laugh. "Plans that will make you wish also that he had killed you."

He grabbed her lapels and pulled her up to a sitting position. "Are you too good to talk to me?" he demanded, his face so close she could smell the garlic on his breath. She closed her eyes.

"Leave her alone, Jean-Jacques!" said St. Pierre from the doorway.

The servant threw her back down on the bed, and Chastity groaned. Jean-Jacques stalked out of the room, and St. Pierre entered, sitting beside her on the narrow cot.

"You must forgive my man; he is very protective of me. I've brought you a cold compress for your face. It should help the pain."

"Why?" croaked Chastity, sucking in sharply as the cold cloth touched her bruised cheek.

"I am French, after all, mademoiselle, and I appreciate beauty. Yours has been, ah, damaged."

"So you want me to look beautiful before you kill me."

St. Pierre stood up and took a turn around the room before speaking. Looking down on her, he said, "I hope that killing *you* will not be necessary."

Chastity managed to sit up so she would not be at such a disadvantage. Although this started her head throbbing horribly again, she said, "If you think for one minute I would have anything to do with you, especially after you harm Alex, you are insane, monsieur. I will kill myself first," she added dramatically before collapsing against the pillow.

She had made him angry, she knew. Would he hit her again? She smiled wryly; her mother always warned her that her tongue would get her into trouble.

"If that is how you feel, mademoiselle, so be it. In the meantime, you will stay in here—bait or hostage, whichever you prefer to call it. You cannot escape, and I will not be so foolish as I was the last time. Good night."

He closed the door with a loud slam, causing Chastity to wince in pain. She allowed her eyes to adjust to the light provided by the large crack under the door. At least she wasn't in total darkness.

She stayed where she was for a few more minutes before forcing herself to sit up. There was only one window, if one could call it that. It was more of a slit at the top of one wall; there would be no chance for escape that way.

The only other opening was the door, and beyond that were St. Pierre and Jean-Jacques. So that was out, too.

Chastity's stomach growled, and she realized it had been twenty-four hours since she had eaten last night's supper in her room before going to the Simpkins' ball. It seemed like a lifetime ago; it had certainly been in a different world. She didn't even have any water, thanks to the fact that she had used the pitcher as a weapon against St. Pierre's hard head.

Chastity went to the door and found it locked, of course. She knocked and said as loudly as she could, "Hello! monsieur, please open the door."

"Stand back," came the harsh reply.

Chastity did as she was bid, shrinking against the far

wall. The door opened and St. Pierre stood there with a pistol trained on her.

"What do you want?" he asked.

She could smell the food they were eating and sniffed the air. "Could I have something to eat and drink? I'm starving."

"Let her starve," growled Jean-Jacques from the room beyond.

But St. Pierre said, "Bring her a plate. And a glass of wine."

"Is there any water?" asked Chastity, her voice pleading the way she had heard her sisters speak when they wanted to get their way from a man.

"And water," added St. Pierre, ignoring the grumbling servant.

"Do you think you could let me have a lamp?" she asked as the plate and glass were brought in and set on the dresser.

But she had gone too far, and St. Pierre said definitely, "No. I don't want you using that to knock one of us out."

"Then could you leave the door open a little? Just while I'm eating."

"Close it and lock her up," said Jean-Jacques.

St. Pierre turned and said fiercely, "Enough of your advice, old woman. I'll do as I please."

He nodded to Chastity and backed away. Chastity pulled the straight-backed chair up to the dresser and began eating with relish. She leaned forward to peek into the other room. There was St. Pierre, watching the door as he continued to eat, the pistol beside his plate. Chastity sat back and finished her meal.

When the servant had removed her plate, St. Pierre reappeared at the door.

"Feeling better?"

"Yes, thank you," said Chastity, still using her little-girl voice. No need to antagonize him; he seemed to be getting more relaxed and mellow. Perhaps she would find a way to escape yet!

"Good," he said gruffly. Then he closed the door and locked it, leaving Chastity in near-darkness again.

She laid down on the cot, turned her face to the wall, and began to cry. Five minutes later, she sat up and dried her eyes. She held her head in her hands and waited for the throbbing brought on by her spate of self-pity to abate.

She never cried, she thought. Oh, when someone died, perhaps. But never for herself. She had long ago decided that it did no good to give in to self-pity. And the tears had only made her headache worse, she realized, rubbing her temples.

But now it was out of the way. She would go to sleep and get a good night's rest. And tomorrow, she would find a way to escape.

Alex waited two hours and then noticed that the clouds were beginning to break up. The last thing he needed was a clear night, with or without a moon. Slowly, he began the ascent.

The heavy iron gate was down, and the door beside it was locked and solid. He looked inside the courtyard and saw a carriage. It might not be the one St. Pierre had taken Chastity away in, but it looked very much like it. The house, he noted, was dark except for one room; if a family lived there, would it not be more likely that several of the rooms would be occupied? he asked himself.

Of course, this was France. Things were not necessarily normal in these times when houses were being taken from their rightful owners and given to the favorites of Napoleon's court.

Alex jumped back as he saw the door to the barn open. The dwarf Jean-Jacques stepped out, whistling softly. He hurried across the courtyard through the rain, and disappeared into the house.

Feeling almost lighthearted, Alex took his knife and tried to force the lock on the door. Unfortunately, the only way the lock would give way was if he shot it with his musket, but that would put Chastity in danger.

Shaking his head, he turned and slid down the embankment to the moat. Thanks to the rain, the water in it was knee-deep. Alex reflected wryly that it was fortunate he was already soaked to the skin. He couldn't get any more uncomfortable.

The moat was overgrown with brambles and trees. Most of these were small, but as he circled the compound, he found one that was as tall as the wall. He put down his musket, made certain his pistols were securely tucked into his belt, and began to climb.

Toward the top, the branches were getting thin and wobbly, and he moved carefully, testing each hand-and foothold. Finally, he was even with the top of the wall, but the shape of the tree, being smaller at the top, had taken him farther away from the wall.

Why had he not thought to bring some rope? Alex asked himself, frustrated and angry. He turned, causing the top of the tree to sway dangerously. He paused thoughtfully; it might be the only way.

A fresh body of black clouds was rolling in, bringing more rain. Alex welcomed the rumbling thunder and cracks of lightning. St. Pierre and Jean-Jacques were unlikely to venture outside in this kind of weather.

Alex moved down one step to a sturdier branch, and, standing on this, he began to move his body back and forth, much like the pumping of a swing. The tree moved back and forth, closer and closer to the wall. The only trouble, he realized dismally, was that he was too low. There was no hope for it; he would have to jump. They might very well find him dead with a broken neck in the morning. Or drowned in the moat's knee-deep water.

Alex took a deep breath, continuing to pump the tree back and forth. With a mighty leap, he pushed off the branch, grasping desperately for the wall. His left hand made contact; his right dangled worthlessly. Swinging by his left arm, Alex brought his right hand up and caught the top of the wall. He hung there resting, as best he could for a moment. Then with a Herculean effort, he swung his leg over the top, and was soon straddling the wall.

Leaning over it as if it were a faithful horse's neck, he hugged it thankfully. He waited for his racing heart to calm before dismounting and making his way along the parapet. The stones were in poor condition, and twice he had to catch himself to keep from falling into the courtyard. He was directly behind the house when he found the stairs and descended to ground level.

Alex circled the house cautiously. He knew almost any noise he made would be put down to the storm, but he also knew that the lightning would show his presence like daylight if St. Pierre or Jean-Jacques were keeping watch. He kept close to the buildings.

Alex went into the barn to get out of the rain. He took out his pistols, reloading them with dry powder, an action so familiar, he didn't need any light. He checked to make sure his knife was still tucked inside his boot.

Then he retraced his steps to the house. The windows were leaded glass, and dirty—impossible to see through clearly. Still, Alex stood outside the lighted room, watching for any sign of movement. He identified two figures in this manner and then frowned. Where was Chastity? If they had shut her into another room, then he might have a chance to kill both of the Frenchmen before they could get to her. It was a very big "if."

If he waited until daylight, there was no telling what might happen to Chastity during the interim. St. Pierre was an evil man; if he took a fancy to Chastity . . .

The door opened, and Alex pressed himself against the wall of the house. It was Jean-Jacques; in his hand was a pistol.

"The horses are fine," he was complaining. "The gate is down, and the Englishman is too stupid even to find us."

"Check anyway!" yelled St. Pierre from the cozy parlor before he slammed the door.

"And he calls me an old woman," griped Jean-Jacques. He ducked his head against the rain and hurried to the barn, not looking in Alex's direction.

Alex followed silently.

The old barn was cold and noisy, wheezing in the wind of the storm. Jean-Jacques had not bothered to close the door, and Alex slipped inside silently.

The servant set the pistol down on the feed trough and gave a hearty pat to the neck of one of the horses. "Old woman, eh? He's the one. Nervous as a cat. Did I not tell him so? You're just fine."

Alex closed in, his knife ready. Jean-Jacques turned, his eyes widening with recognition. He whirled for the pistol, but Alex was too quick for him. The little man ducked down, scrambling between Alex's legs, almost getting away. Alex grabbed his ankle and pulled him back. He raised his fist and punched the servant in the jaw. Jean-Jacques kicked upward, incapacitating Alex long enough to run back for the gun. Alex ignored the pain and flew at the dwarf, knocking him to the ground again. After giving a great whoosh of breath, the servant lay still.

Alex pulled Jean-Jacques's body away from the

horse's hoofs and listened for a pulse. The man was barely breathing. Looking around for some rope, Alex tied him up.

Then he waited.

He hoped St. Pierre had not ordered the servant to sleep in the barn. It was essential that St. Pierre miss his servant and come looking for him. Alex lighted a lantern of welcome. The rain, too, was playing into his hands as it slowed to a mere drizzle.

Almost a half an hour passed before he saw the door to the house open cautiously. From his hiding place, Alex could see St. Pierre's expression in the light from the open door. He could almost hear the man's thoughts. Then the Frenchman seemed to come to a decision, comforted, no doubt, by the lantern lighting the barn. He would be thinking that no one who wished to surprise him would have lighted the lantern.

And he would be wrong, thought Alex, his excitement growing.

St. Pierre walked across the yard, his pistol tucked safely in his belt, his arms swinging freely at his sides.

"Jean-Jacques!" he called.

Alex waited until the man had entered the barn before he rose, his gun aimed between the man's eyes, and said, "Drop the gun, St. Pierre."

With a desperate gleam in his eyes, St. Pierre whirled to face him. Alex had seen the look before, on the battlefield, when his opponent knew all was lost and made the decision to die fighting.

St. Pierre went for his pistol, and Alex fired. St. Pierre fell to the ground, his gun discharging harmlessly into the air.

Alex checked to be sure he was dead before he turned to the house. As he entered the front hall, he paused. He had assumed there were no other servants. What if some of the smugglers who had escaped had come here, too?

He proceeded more cautiously, stepping into the darkened room on the right first. It was empty. The entire house was silent. Then he turned into the room on the left, the room where there was a fire and lamps were lighted. There was no one there. He knew it unlikely anyone else was in the house since all the other rooms were dark.

Then he heard a sound that set his hair on end. It was the sound of something being dragged. He listened, his gaze traveling to the closed door on the other side of the room.

Gripping his loaded pistol more tightly, he moved closer. The sound continued, but it was different now, as if something heavier was being moved.

He tried the door, but it was locked. He saw a key on the mantel and picked it up, pushing it into the keyhole and turning it slowly.

He lifted the handle and pushed, but something was blocking the doorway.

"Damn," he said softly.

"Alex? Alex, is that you?" asked Chastity, her breathing labored.

"Chastity, open the door!" he called.

"I will," she said, her tone giddy. "I moved all the furniture against the door when I heard the shot."

He could hear her struggling to clear the door.

"Get back," he said, gathering his strength. With a mighty shove, he pushed back the bed and chest and slipped inside.

Sobbing with joy, Chastity fell into his arms, kissing him, clutching him to her breast.

After a few minutes, Alex looked down into her eyes. "Glad to see me?"

She pushed him away playfully, but didn't let go.

Looking toward the open door, she asked solemnly, "Are they dead?"

"St. Pierre, yes. The other one, I'm not sure. He was still breathing." Chastity shivered and clung to him even tighter. "It's alright, my love; I tied him up. Let's get out of here. I hate to ride in the dark, but without the carriage, we might just be able to make it back to the rendezvous tonight."

"Rendezvous?" she asked, giving him her hand as he helped her climb over the furniture and into the light.

"Humphries is supposed to be there every night to pick us up."

"Every night?" asked Chastity, tugging at her skirt and smoothing her hair. She had removed the jacket of her riding habit earlier and now put it back on, wrinkling her nose at the smell of damp wool.

Alex took her hands with his own as he said quietly, "For three nights."

Chastity nodded as they acknowledged to each other how close they had come to disaster.

"Let's go. At least it's stopped raining."

They crossed the courtyard and entered the barn. Chastity averted her face when they had to step over the body of St. Pierre. She followed Alex to the first stall, pausing and looking at the floor as he had.

Alex spun around, expecting the attack to come from behind. Instead, it came from above, as Jean-Jacques leapt from the rafters and knocked him to the ground.

Chastity screamed, jumping back from the two men wrestling desperately in the straw. She looked around for a weapon and picked up a pitchfork.

Then she stood helplessly as the two bodies struggled, making it impossible for her to use her weapon. Jean-Jacques had wrapped a length of rusty chain around his fist and was beating Alex unmercifully. But Alex was larger and managed to throw the smaller man off him.

As the dwarf resumed the attack, Alex rolled to one side and sprang to his feet.

Chastity screamed his name and tossed him the pitchfork. When Jean-Jacques leapt forward, he impaled himself on the deadly tines.

Alex dropped the pitchfork and stood there, his eyes closed, his face bruised and bleeding. Stepping past the dead man, Chastity took him in her arms and gently kissed him.

"Can we go now?" she asked.

Alex nodded. They put bridles on the two carriage horses and led them outside.

"I suppose I should bury them," said Alex doubtfully. "Their bodies aren't likely to be discovered by anyone else."

"I don't know, Alex, there was a man here when we arrived. I got the feeling he would be coming back to check on things. He left when he found out the English militia might be coming after me. He was none too pleased with the way St. Pierre had managed things."

"Who was he?" asked Alex eagerly. "Could you describe him?"

"He was from the upper class; I could tell that much by his clothes and his accent. St. Pierre called him 'Talley,' but the man cut him off, so I don't know if that was his full name or not. He seemed anxious that St. Pierre not use his name."

Alex grinned and said, "You just may have met one of the most powerful men in France today, my dear. Unless I miss my guess, that was Talleyrand. He likes to keep his finger on everything, including their intelligence. I would have liked to capture him!"

"Well, I'm glad you didn't! That would have meant one more man for you to get by!" said Chastity tartly.

Alex laughed and said obediently, "Yes, dear," before

helping her to mount. "Think you can manage astride and bareback?" he asked.

Chastity threw him a look of disdain and kicked the horse, sending him toward the open gate at a jolting trot. She clutched tightly with her knees and held onto the mane, but she didn't disgrace herself.

Chapter Ten

They rode down the hill, pausing at the bottom to turn and look back. Chastity shivered and Alex put his hand over hers.

"I'm alright; only tired," she said.

"It won't be long now and you can have a good sleep."

"How far is the boat?"

"About two hours by horseback, I should think. Would you rather ride with me?" he asked.

Chastity shook her head, smiling. "No, I'll make it. You just lead the way, and we'll follow," she said, patting her nag's neck.

Back down the side road to the path that ran parallel to the Channel they went, Alex in the lead. Chastity swayed from time to time, but she was determined to make it back to the boat. She wouldn't feel safe until they reached England.

The sky was turning a muddy gray by the time they reached the beach. It was deserted, and so was the water in front of it.

"I guess we've missed our ride," said Alex, trying to make light of their situation.

Chastity heaved a sigh and slipped to the ground. "What now?"

Alex looked around at the desolate beach and pointed to a small crescent-shaped hollow which had a few paltry trees. We'll tether the horses there and try to get some sleep. We'll be out of the wind, and I'll see if I can get a fire going to warm you up a bit."

"Do you think we should?" asked Chastity.

"Why not?"

She was so weary, she wasn't sure she could say what had to be said. But she took a deep breath and said candidly, "Because this is where the smugglers meet their boats. And it is probably known by now that we escaped. Won't they begin their search for us here?"

"I don't think . . ." began Alex bluffly.

"Yes, you do. That's why you want us off the beach, why you want to tether the horses instead of letting them go. You're thinking we may need them to travel or to sell for our passage. Wouldn't it be ironic if we had to smuggle ourselves home!" Her voice had increased in volume and broke on the word "home."

Alex gathered her into his arms to comfort her. When she had regained her composure, she pushed away, wiping her tears.

"I promise you, Alex, I don't do that all the time."

"Good, because I can't stand to see you cry. Now, come on. Things could be worse. We've been lucky so far; we'll come about."

As he spoke, he led her and the horses to the hollowed-out hill that faced the beach. It would provide good shelter, and Chastity sank down on the sand gratefully. Alex looked at a fallen branch, but he had to admit he didn't like the idea of a fire. The smoke might attract attention.

"I wish I had thought to take some blankets from the house," Alex said, using his coat to rub down the horses. "But we can't think of everything, can we?"

He turned around when there was no answer and

smiled. Chastity was sound asleep, curled up on the sand, her head resting on a tuft of grass. Alex finished with the animals and joined Chastity. He leaned against one of the trees and pulled her closer, cradling her head in his lap. He placed his pistols beside him and closed his eyes.

The sun was high when he awoke. He was lying on the sand, too, with Chastity curled snugly up against him. He looked around as best he could without disturbing her. All appeared to be normal, and he closed his eyes again.

When Alex next opened his eyes, he found Chastity had turned and was watching him. He smiled and kissed the tip of her nose.

"Happy Christmas," he said.

"Happy Christmas?" she echoed in surprise. "I'd forgotten all about what day it was."

"You never did tell me if you liked your Christmas present," he said, touching the pendant that still hung around her neck.

"I love it, but you were awful to let me go on believing it was for the comtesse, when all the while . . ."

He grinned. "Yes, for that lovely comtesse."

"And you knew all the while that *she* was a *he*, didn't you!"

"Almost all the time."

Chastity pursed her lips and frowned. "When did you discover it?"

"On one of my forays into St. Pierre's house."

"Yes, but when? Was it before or after that picnic?" she asked suspiciously.

Alex laughed. "Don't tell me you're going to be jealous of a man?" When she didn't respond, he said, "Very well, I think it was before the picnic that I found out for certain."

"So all that feeding her—I mean him—of strawberries was . . ."

"Was to find out more information from her—I mean him," said Alex, his own temper being tried. They frowned at each other for another minute before Alex shook his head, saying, "This is stupid. Even if St. Pierre had been a woman, I was never attracted to the comtesse. How could I have been when I was falling in love with you?"

Chastity dropped her eyes, smiling slightly. Then Alex lifted her chin and kissed her on the lips.

Sitting up suddenly, he said briskly, "Enough of that for now! I'll see if I can find something for breakfast."

Chastity sat up and stretched. Then she excused herself and disappeared on the other side of the rise. Alex rose, too, on the alert for any danger that might present itself. He relaxed when Chastity came back into view.

Alex strolled down the beach and then walked inland for a short distance. He found a patch of wild berries, overripe, but edible. He also pulled up some rather meager wild carrots.

He returned to the beach and offered Chastity his finds. "It's not much, but it will help keep us from starving," he said.

She took a handful of berries and looked up at the sky, asking, "About what time is it?"

"I'd say around four o'clock. It will be dark soon. We slept all day."

"And I'm still tired. Oh, for a good hot bath and a soft bed." She blushed and turned away when Alex grinned at her.

He went to her and took her hands. "You needn't be shy with me, Chastity. Not now." Intending to put her at ease, he asked, "Tell me what kind of wedding you would like. Something big and fancy? Perhaps St. Paul's in London, with all the world invited?"

Chastity shook her head. "No, Alex, surely you know me better than that. Just a quiet ceremony at the village church. That's all I want."

Alex frowned. "It needn't be quite so insignificant as that, surely. As for me, I've a mind to shout it from the rooftops, not skulk about like thieves, being wed in some ramshackle, clandestine ceremony."

Chastity bowed her head. How could she explain to him about her past? For once, she wished he knew; she didn't think she could bear to tell him. She was not that brave.

"Chastity? What's wrong?"

"I just think it might not be a good idea, for me, that is, to act quite so ... flamboyantly."

Alex shook his head. "Is it flamboyant to want to share our happiness with everyone?"

"No," she said softly.

"If you think what happened years ago would make me any less proud to be marrying you, Chastity, then tell me now. I won't have that coming between us."

"Then you know?" she asked.

"Of course I know. First that fool Charlie told me some nonsense which I didn't believe. Don't forget, I had kissed you and knew you were not some lightskirt. And then I heard the truth from your own lips."

Chastity frowned, saying, "But I have never talked about it to anyone."

"Yes, you did. To your sisters the other day on the terrace." He grinned and added, "I was eavesdropping. One hears the most astounding things."

"Oh, Alex," she sighed. "How can you want to marry me?"

"How? Because I love you, you silly wench, and I would be miserable without you. Chastity," he said, pulling her close, "you're too intelligent to think a kiss or two could possibly make you . . . I don't know what you're thinking . . . unworthy?"

She sobbed and tried to tear away from him, for that was exactly what she was thinking. But he held her tight.

"I don't care what your mother has told you; she was simply being absurd."

"But Alex, I did kiss Winchester. And we were alone—at Vauxhall. We had gotten separated from our group, and he wanted to sit down to rest. When . . . I just wanted to see what it was like." Her tone changed to self-mockery as she added, "And I didn't even like it!"

Alex laughed at this and took her face in his hands, kissing her with more passion than he had yet allowed himself. Chastity swayed against him weakly, returning his kiss with ardor.

"There," said Alex hoarsely as he released her. "Did you enjoy that?" She only nodded. "Then I don't want to ever hear another word about your past. I love you, and you love me, and that is all that matters. And if your sainted mother makes one comment, one intimation, the least bit disparaging, send her to me." He looked her in the eye and said solemnly, "Promise?"

"I promise."

"How touching!" drawled a voice from above.

Chastity would have leapt back, but Alex held her close, his hand coming between them as he removed his pistol from his belt.

He looked up into the setting sun and saw only a silhouette.

"Bonjour, monsieur," he called, using his best French. "I'm afraid you have me at a disadvantage. Allow me to introduce myself. My name is Alexander Fitzsimmons. And yours?"

The man gave a mirthless laugh and Alex drew his pistol, shoving Chastity to one side.

The silhouette stopped laughing and said, "Do you think I am alone, Mr. Fitzsimmons? I did guess, you see, that if you were able to kill St. Pierre, then you would be a worthy opponent. I was not so foolish as to come alone! Denis! Andre!"

There was a struggle to his right, and Chastity screamed. Alex never flinched, keeping his pistol trained on the silhouette.

"Let her go, or I'll kill him," Alex said quietly.

"Ow!" yelped a deep voice beside him.

"Let me go!" shouted Chastity, aiming another backward kick and connecting with a resounding thud.

"Ow!" said her captor, throwing her to the ground.

Alex glanced over and said, "Chastity, get behind me. You! Andre or Denis, whichever you are. If you touch her, I'll kill your commander up there. Stand back!"

The silhouette signalled the two men to move back. Just then a loud boom sounded, and sand exploded down the beach.

"It's Humphries!" shouted Chastity. "They're coming ashore!"

"Go out to the boat, Chastity," ordered Alex, his stance never wavering.

"Not without you," she said vehemently.

"Yes, without me. I'll be there in a minute. Now do as I say. Just this once." With his free hand, he gave her a little push.

"Alex," she whispered.

"Go on. I'll be careful."

Chastity backed toward the approaching dinghy. She heard it scrape the sand and turned around, calling back to Alex, "It's here, Alex. Come on!"

Men in red coats passed her, muskets at the ready. Chastity was drawn into the boat.

"What will it be?" said Alex. "It's your call, monsieur."

"Then I say we will meet again, some other time, Mr. Fitzsimmons. I hate to distress you, but you are not worth my life." With that, he vanished down the other side of the hill.

"Shall we go after him, Captain?" asked the lieutenant.

Alex turned and grinned at Humphries. "No, and let those two go as well. We've done enough already."

"Let them go, men," said the lieutenant. He held out his hand to Alex. "Glad you could make it, sir. Happy Christmas."

"Happy Christmas," said Alex, walking toward the small boat. Chastity waited where she was, accepting his embrace with relief. "Let's go home, Lieutenant."

Chastity slept during the crossing, her exhaustion and relief at being safe colliding and sent her into a deep sleep. She had cleaned up and changed into one of the sailor's uniforms. It was much too big on her slender form, but Alex thought she looked beautiful with her hair brushed and plaited down her back. They had put her in the Petershams' cabin, but she never noticed her luxurious surroundings. Alex sat beside her bed, but he didn't sleep.

By the time they arrived back at Hartford House, they would cause quite a stir. They had been gone since the night of the twenty-third and wouldn't get back to Dover, where the yacht was to dock, until tomorrow, the twenty-sixth. Her family was probably frantic, but that wouldn't stave off Lady Hartford's attack. He didn't think Chastity would be up to it.

Quietly, he left her and went up on the deck to speak to the captain of the ship. "Captain, I was wondering if I could persuade you to make a slight detour."

"Where to, Mr. Fitzsimmons?"

"There's a shallow cove between Folkestone and Dover. If you could see your way clear to sail there directly, I could get Miss Hartford home without so much fuss."

"She's all done in, I'll be bound," said the captain, his own daughters coming to mind.

"She is that, sir," agreed Alex, allowing the captain to reach his own decision.

"Very well, Mr. Fitzsimmons. Could you be a little more precise about the spot where you wish us to set you ashore?"

"Certainly," said Alex, giving directions to the navigator.

"Chastity, wake up, darling," said Alex, prodding her gently. "We're home. We've just got to go ashore," he added as she lolled against his shoulder. "Come on; wake up."

"We're home?" she mumbled as if she had been drugged.

"That's right. Now come along." Half-carrying her and half dragging her, Alex managed to get her into the dinghy.

Shaking hands with Lieutenant Humphries and returning his salute, he said, "You've got my report. Tell them in London I'll be up in a day or two to fill in the details."

"Yes, sir," said Humphries, swelling with pride.

"Thank you, Captain," said Alex, turning to the ship's officer. "Couldn't have managed any of this without you and your boat. You've done your country a great service." Here again, Alex received and returned a snappy salute.

The sailors rowing the small boat soon had them on the beach, and Alex helped Chastity out. He shook hands with James and Henry, who had also come ashore, and bid them good-bye.

"Alex, I'm scared," Chastity said, coming out of her stupor.

"Of what? It's after midnight. All of the house party guests will have left by now. Your family will doubtless all be exhausted and in their beds. We can slip in without anyone being the wiser and get a good night's sleep before . . . Well, before we have to explain anything."

"How diplomatically phrased," she managed to say.

"You know I'm right. Come along, Miss Hartford. I'll walk you to your room." He held out his arm, and she took it, leaning on him heavily.

It was as Alex had predicted except that the servants were not all in bed. Cook and Petrie were sitting at the kitchen table with two cups of tea and a bottle of brandy between them. When the back door opened, they sprang to life, demanding to know everything.

"Not tonight," said Alex firmly, supporting Chastity with a possessive arm around her waist.

"But Mr. Fitzsimmons," breathed Cook. "My Jane . . ."

"Is she alright?" asked Chastity quickly.

"Yes, and the babe, too. My other daughter is with her tonight."

"Good, then she'll be there when James gets home."

"Then he's not dead?"

"Not dead and none the worse for wear, Cook," said Alex, pushing past. "He's a brave lad, but we'll let him tell you all about that. Right now, I'm going to get Miss Chastity into her own bed."

"Oh, let me, Mr. Fitzsimmons," said the cook, trying to take over.

Chastity shook her head. "Alex can take care of me, Cook. You go on to bed—both of you." She managed a smile for them and let Alex help her to the stairs.

When they reached her room, Alex opened the door

quitely. A fire burned in the grate despite the lateness of the hour.

"Well, someone was thinking about welcoming you home," he said, leading her to the bed. "Let me tuck you up, young lady."

But when the covers were securely around her, Chastity wouldn't let him go, holding his hand in fevered desperation.

"Please, Alex, don't go. I don't want to be alone. What if I wake up and it was all a dream?"

He picked up the pendant that lay across her breast and studied it thoughtfully. "You know it was all real, Chastity. I'm not going to go away."

"I know," she said weakly. "But I don't want you to leave me tonight. Please."

She sounded like her sisters engaged in their most appealing whining, but she didn't care. She watched him with wide eyes.

Alex smiled and smoothed her hair. He leaned over and kissed her brow. "Alright, my love, I'll stay, but I'm deuced if I'll spend another night sitting up. Move over."

Chastity scooted to the other side of the bed, and Alex climbed on top of the covers, keeping well on his side.

"Coward," said a small voice from the other side of the bed.

"Vixen."

Walking the floors like a zombie, Lady Hartford would wring her hands, dab her eyes with a lace handkerchief, and take a whiff of her smelling salts from time to time, her maid trailing along behind her like a shadow.

"Divinity, you're not doing yourself any good behaving in this way," said Lord Hartford, who also showed signs of exhaustion and worry.

"Leave me alone, Herbert. You don't know how a mother feels," she moaned delicately. "Each time I pass her room, I go inside and wonder what might have happened. If only . . . But it is too . . ."

The scream that followed would have awakened the dead, and even her husband and maid, accustomed to her dramatics, were startled. They peered inside the bedroom, their mouths dropping open at the sight that met their eyes.

Alex sat up, rubbing the sleep from his eyes, trying to focus on the cause of the disturbance.

Chastity, sitting up beside him, blinked hard and whispered, "Mother!"

Lord Hartford moved into the room, dragging his prostrate wife and her hysterical maid with him. He slapped the maid and took the smelling salts, waving them energetically beneath Lady Hartford's nose. With a groan, she pushed his hand away and straightened up.

"Chastity Hartford! What is the . . ."

"Divinity! Shut your mouth!"

"But Herbert!"

"For once in your life, Divinity, let me handle this!" he snapped angrily. Lady Hartford accepted her maid's help and settled into the nearest chair.

"Alex," said his lordship with a casual nod.

"My lord," said Alex, his mischievous sense of humor getting the best of him. He swung his bare feet to the floor and stood up. He was glad he had resisted temptation and stayed above the covers, but he said, "You did give me your permission, my lord."

Lord Hartford almost choked, and Chastity giggled.

"Chastity!" said her mother.

"Be quiet, Divinity," ordered her father. Lord Hartford rocked on his heels and said, "I did have in mind a wedding ceremony first, Alex."

"And if we'd had a special license and a rector, believe me, we would have taken advantage of them. But unfortunately, we've been a little busy for that."

"Did you catch them?" asked Chastity's father, unable to mask his excitement.

"Herbert!"

Alex nodded. "They're all taken care of, but it's been a difficult time, and Chastity is exhausted. Why don't I go downstairs with you and explain."

"No, Alex, I want you to stay with me," said Chastity, causing her mother to swoon again.

Lord Hartford gave his wife a cursory glance before nodding. "Very well, Chastity, have it your way." He turned to Alex and said, "I'll take her ladyship to her room. And then, with your permission, I'll send over to Canterbury. I'm well acquainted with the bishop, and I think I can get him to write out a special license."

"But Papa, nothing happened," said Chastity, giving him a warning frown.

He walked across the room to her side of the bed and kissed her brow. "I know that, my girl. Now, and before. I just never wanted to make the effort before to stand up to your mother. Now, you and Alex, you go back to sleep. I'll make sure you're not disturbed. We can talk about the wedding later."

"Thank you, Papa."

Left alone again, Chastity looked at Alex shyly.

"That wasn't so bad," he said, smiling at her.

"No, but you really are a dreadful man, teasing Papa like that."

"What do you mean?"

"About his giving his permission . . . for this."

Alex climbed back onto the bed, propping himself up on one elbow and leaning over her. "But he did give me permission. Not that I needed it. You're the only one I'll ever ask permission of. May I?" he asked. She nodded, and he kissed her.

Turning over on his back, he groaned. "This is very challenging," he said.

"Why? I've said you may," said Chastity, raising up and snuggling against him.

"Chastity, Chastity, Chastity. How did you ever get a name like that?" he demanded of the ceiling, before a pillow came crashing down on his head.

Epilogue

"Alex!" called Chastity as she entered his dressing room. She looked beyond her husband, who was putting the finishing touches on his cravat, to Alex's valet. His expression of consternation caused her to smile; on the dressing table was a pile of ruined cravats. "Having a difficult time of it?" she asked airily.

The valet frowned at such a frivolous inquiry about the all-important task his master had just accomplished, but he held his peace.

Alex grinned at Chastity and dismissed his man with a wave of the hand. The valet shook his head dolefully as he withdrew, knowing his master's perfect cravat was about to go the way so many others had when his mistress entered the dressing room.

"What is it, my love?" Alex asked, drawing her to him.

Chastity was clad in a sensible lawn wrapper, her hair still down. She waved a note under his nose.

"It's from Mother. She's had another row with Cook and wants me to come and smooth things over for her. I'll have to meet you at their house."

"Why don't we just pretend we never received the note? For that matter, never received the invitation to this gala ball."

Chastity shook her head and said dryly, "That would be rather difficult since Mother has planned the ball to publicly, albeit belatedly, announce our marriage to all of London society."

"The fact that she was already giving the ball to present Tranquility and Sincerity to the *Ton* couldn't have anything to do with it," said Alex, leaning closer and kissing her ear lightly.

"Now, Alex," she said, tilting her head to one side to allow him access to her neck. Alex accepted her invitation, and they were soon oblivious to time, and notes, and in-laws.

Almost two hours had passed before they presented themselves at the Hartford's townhouse. Chastity's mother gave her a tight-lipped welcome, but her father slapped Alex on the back and kissed his favorite daughter before sending them through to the ballroom.

Pretending to watch the dancers, Alex placed his mouth close to Chastity's ear and whispered, "You notice your mother didn't ask why we were so late."

Chastity giggled and said, "I didn't think she would, not after last time when you told her exactly what had taken us so long."

"You must admit, it effectively put a stop to all her personal inquiries. And a good thing, too, else I wouldn't have been able to tolerate living so close to her, no matter how much I might like my godparents' old home."

"I know. By the way, did you remember to tell James to send word when the mare foaled?"

"Yes, he'll let us know."

"Good evening, Miss Chastity, Alex," said Ruben Oxworth, his eyes only darting in their direction before he returned his attention to the dancers.

"Hello, Mr. Oxworth. I didn't know you had come to town."

"Wouldn't miss it. Have you seen your sister? Do you know what color her dress is?"

"Probably a sprigged muslin, just like all the other young ladies. There she is, with Sir Charles."

"Ah, yes. Doesn't she look exceptionally pretty tonight?" said the smitten older man. "If you'll excuse me ..." The music was ending, and they watched as Ruben made his way toward Tranquility.

"He's got it bad, poor fellow," said Alex. "Care to dance?"

"I'd love to," said Chastity, watching Tranquility shake her head to Ruben Oxworth, pointing to her dance card. Then Tranquility turned and took the hand of another young man, her face animated as she laughed at some witticism. Ruben Oxworth turned on his heel and stalked toward the refreshment room.

"I'm afraid Tranquility has decided against Ruben," said Chastity.

"So it would seem; it was an unlikely match, to say the least."

"I know, but I hate to see anyone hurt," said Chastity before the motions of the dance separated them.

When they came back together, Chastity continued, "Perhaps we can introduce him to someone else, someone more suitable."

"Someone less likely to wreak havoc on his quiet life," added Alex cynically.

"True. I wonder if ..."

"No," said Alex, shaking his head and frowning down at her. "You don't need to get involved."

"But Alex, I want everyone to be as happy as I am," said Chastity, giving him a coquettish smile. Again the steps of the dance separated them, and Chastity put her mind to finding a suitable match for Ruben Oxworth.

"Do you think he might like . . ."

"No, Chastity, I don't. And I don't want you worrying about Oxworth. You've got enough to think about between me and little Persnickety."

Chastity gurgled with laughter. "Persnickety?" she said. "His name will be something sensible and simple like John or Susan."

"I doubt *he* would like being named Susan," murmured Alex, and Chastity rapped him playfully on the arm with her fan.

She sighed, wishing the long set would end. Her face must have proclaimed her weariness, because Alex pulled her from the dance floor unceremoniously. He led her to a secluded alcove and seated her on a velvet loveseat.

"We should have stayed in bed," he said, his voice taking on the tones of a governess.

Chastity shook her head. "I'll be fine; it was just going on so long."

"I'll get you some punch," he said, starting off toward the refreshment room.

"Chastity! What was that about?"

Chastity looked up to face her mother. "It was nothing, Mother. I simply got a little tired."

"Tired? From one set? I thought you knew better than to leave a dance floor like that."

"I'm sorry, Mother. I . . ."

"If you wish to berate someone, Lady Hartford, berate me. I took her off the floor. Anyone could see she was all done in."

Lady Hartford stood up, her son-in-law's veiled disparagement of her motherly instincts making her uncomfortable. But then, she often found herself uncomfortable in his company. He was always quick to defend Chastity against the slightest admonishment.

Chastity accepted the glass of milk Alex had requested from Cook.

With a frown, Lady Hartford looked from the liquid to Chastity, to Alex, and back to Chastity. "Aren't you going to explain this?"

Alex smiled at Chastity. "What do you think, my love? Should we explain it?"

Chastity obviously didn't wish to do so, but she saw no hope for it. She knew her mother would not be put off with some prevarication.

"Very well. Mother, you are going to be a grandmother come next autumn. Mother!"

Chastity leapt to her feet to help Alex catch her mother, who had swooned. A small crowd began to gather. Lady Hartford's maid appeared with her smelling salts, bringing her back to consciousness. Her husband had left the card room and was kneeling down beside her. She clutched at his lapels.

"A grandmother, a grandmother . . ." she moaned. "I'm not ready to be a grandmother."

"Grandmother?" said Lord Hartford, looking up at Chastity. Her smile told him everything, and he embraced his daughter across his wife's prone body. "Grandpa! How marvelous! Congratulations, my boy!" he said, grasping Alex's hand. He helped Chastity to her feet and announced in a loud voice. "I'm going to be a grandfather!"

Tranquility's and Sincerity's come-out ball had taken a turn for the worse, Lady Hartford observed to her friends, but her guests had a wonderful time, celebrating a wedding and a birth, instead of a simple debut.

At midnight, Alex took Chastity's hand and led her inexorably toward the door and the waiting carriage.

"But Alex, it's only midnight."

"That's right, and I don't want my Cinders turning into a pumpkin. We're going home, all three of us."

They entered the carriage, and he bent down as though conversing with her stomach. "What's that, little Dexterity, you're ready for bed? I thought as much."

"Alex, you are so absurd. I don't know why I ever married you."

"Shall I refresh your memory?" he asked, pulling her onto his lap.

After several breathless kisses, Chastity sighed, "Won't this carriage ever get us home?"

"Impatient, my sweet?"

"Where you are concerned? Always."